Jared's Family

By
V.S. Morgan

Copyright © 2017 by V.S. Morgan
ISBN: 978-1-68361-179-0
Cover art by Tibbs Desgins and
Decadent Publishing LLC

Published by
Decadent Publishing Company, LLC

Look for us online at:
www.decadentpublishing.com

~A Note from the Author~

Dear Readers,

I'm excited to share Virge, Jared, and D with you. They've been in my head and heart long before I actually started writing their story. Family comes in so many forms, and I loved bringing these three together.

In the story, D calls any man "daddy" and any woman "mommy" regardless age (anyone not a child) and race. I based this on my own son doing this at that age. It still warms my heart remembering the happiness and slight confusion on people's faces when he joyfully yelled "Mama!" or "Papa!" to them. And when he couldn't quite it my nickname of Ness right so he called me Mama Nest. LOL!

I'd love to hear what you thought of the story. I can be reached at vs_morgan@yahoo.com

Best,
VS

Dedication

BIG thanks to my readers. I couldn't do this without you!

Chapter One

Jared was going to kill his brother. Taking the stairs two at a time, he prepared to rip Nate a new one. Since his older brother Sam had left early with his wife, Gabi, and their baby, Nate's no-show meant he'd had to do the work of three—mucking out all the stalls and feeding and watering the horses. And the ass munch hadn't even bothered to answer his phone.

Reaching the top of the stairs, he yelled, "Nate, what the fuck, man?"

His righteous anger fizzled at the retching sounds emitting from the bathroom. *Hell.*

The bathroom door opened, and his brother shuffled out. Damn, Nate looked like crap warmed up. His normally supermodel-worthy hair hung limp, his face waxy, and his eyes dull.

Jared steered his brother back to his room. Nate flopped onto his bed with a moan, and Jared left to get a damp rag and a glass of water, which he passed to Nate when he returned.

His brother took a tiny sip of water. "Sorry I

missed chores, bro. Feel like shit."

Jared propped a shoulder against the doorframe. "You look like shit, too."

"Ha ha," Nate said, in a tone as flat as his eyes.

"Why don't you get some rest? I'll take care of stuff around the ranch." They didn't have any guests arriving until tomorrow, so he could manage the rest of the chores without him.

Nate settled against his pillows only to spring up. He groaned and held his head in his hands. "Fuck, I'm supposed to be at the library today."

"Call and cancel."

His brother shook his head. "I can't let the kids down."

"Well, you're not going in sick." He lifted his arm, using his shirt sleeve to swipe the sweat dripping down his forehead.

Jesus, he was too tired for Nate's brand of drama.

His brother's eyes widened, and Jared could almost see a lightbulb glowing above his head. *Shit, that can't be good.*

"You could go in my place!" Nate exclaimed.

"What? Dealing with kids under five isn't in my wheelhouse." Hell, he was still nervous holding his infant niece, Olivia.

"There's nothing to it. You just wear the outfit, read them a few books, and hand out stickers. Heck, you could even sign. The kids would love that."

This could result in a complete clusterfuck, but his brother gave his patented puppy-dog look. Jared rolled his eyes and huffed. "Fine. But I'm not driving to town in that outfit. Likely get in an accident."

"Thanks, man. I owe you one." Nate smiled

weakly.

Jared smirked. "Damn right you do. You going to be okay?"

"Yeah, just going to sleep." His brother turned onto his side, pulling the blankets up to his chin.

"Your trash can is right there, and I'll get Wyatt to check on you while I'm gone." Better their patient eldest brother than Jared. The rarely sick Nate could be a real pain in the ass.

A soft snore sounded.

Jared shook his head and left. Time to shower before facing a horde of little ones. *Yay.*

***

Virge helped D up onto the lobby bench located near the library's entrance. He gave his three-year-old nephew his snack. Checking his phone, he grimaced. In the short trip to the library, he'd received ten messages from his agent.

He didn't want to talk to Miranda right now. While she was phenomenal at her job, he didn't want her bulldog tactics directed at him. His chest tightened, and he glanced down at D to ground himself. *Better get it over with.* Taking a deep breath, he tapped her number. She answered on the first ring.

"Oh, Virge, I'm so glad you returned my call." Miranda's accent was still hardcore New Yorker despite living in L.A. for the last twenty years.

He refrained from correcting her that he'd received calls in the double digits, not just one. "Hey, Miranda. What's up?"

"You need to hire a publicist yesterday. My

phone has been ringing like crazy. Now that *Death in the Dungeon* is in the news for casting, people want to see Malcolm Stone."

He sighed. While he participated in online and print interviews under the pen name of Malcolm Stone, he never used his image, and he didn't attend public events. His publisher had loved the added mystique, but once the movie deal came into play, requests for in-person interviews and photos flooded in.

"I'm still on the force." His captain allowed his "hobby" as long as his identity remained private. The LAPD didn't need a media circus at its door.

"The rumors are circulating again."

He grunted. "I don't care if people think I'm a straight white lady. Having a dick doesn't make me a better writer." Glancing up at a startled "humph," he caught a frown from an elderly man shuffling by with a walker. Virge lowered his voice. "None of my contracts require me to do appearances."

"But, Virge, the fans love you. And think about what it would do for your career. Are you still considering resigning?"

"There's too much going on right now to be making big decisions. I'm focused on D."

His life had imploded in the last four months. Within days of negotiating movie rights for his first three books, his sister died, leaving Virge the guardian of her young son.

Miranda made a sympathetic sound. "How's the new story going?"

Does staring at a blank screen for hours count? "Making some progress," he hedged.

"Tabitha said they're seeing a large spike in

women readers. They *looove* Derek Price. She asked if you'd consider adding a romantic interest. Oh, what about Seth?"

He ran his hand over his close-cropped hair. *Christ, Seth is like a little brother to Derek.* "I'm not sure that's my thing."

He was a single, forty-three-year-old gay man raising a preschooler. Even before D had come to live with him, men were few and far between. Virge didn't do casual hookups, and his erratic work hours eventually drove away all the men he dated. What the hell did he know about writing romance? He'd written some hot sex scenes for his bed-hopping main character, but neither of them had a clue about love.

He missed whatever Miranda said next as his gaze landed on a male vision in leather. The cowboy's spurs jangled as he strode past. This was rural Montana. Who went to the library decked out in a cowboy hat, full-length duster, gloves, chaps, and boots with spurs? The guy should have looked completely ludicrous in that getup, but Virge's immediate impression? *Fucking sexy.* Tall with broad shoulders, the man radiated strength and power. He sat up straighter and stared as the hot cowboy entered the library.

"Virge, are you listening to me?" Miranda's voice grated in his ear.

He flinched, almost dropping his phone. "Yes."

After a few minutes of making noncommittal noises and saying he'd think about her ideas, he ended the call. "Okay, buddy, ready to get some books?"

D had disappeared.

Virge's chest tightened with panic. How had he missed D leaving? The little guy normally stuck to him like glue. *Fuck*. He'd gotten too complacent.

He checked the bathroom across the hall. Empty. He entered the library and stopped at the main desk. "Have you seen my nephew? He's wearing a red shirt, jeans, and carrying a blue teddy bear."

The petite, redheaded woman shook her head and pointed to the left. "Sorry, I haven't. Check the children's area."

He sped in the direction she'd indicated, dodging library patrons in his path, slowing only when he reached the area decorated in bright primary colors and pint-sized furniture. D leaned against the side of a small bookcase, clutching his precious stuffed animal, Boo Bear, at his side.

Oh, thank God. Releasing a breath, Virge sat on the carpet next to D who remained transfixed by the cowboy sitting in a ridiculously tiny chair surrounded by little kids several feet away. A thin, gray-haired woman held a sturdy book while the sexy man both read aloud and signed the story in American Sign Language.

He relaxed, listening to the deep, quiet voice. The man signed with a confidence that spoke of years of use, and Virge wondered if he had a deaf family member. Perhaps a parent? How old was he? Late twenties, early thirties, maybe? His visceral attraction to the Adonis in leather heightened his innate curiosity. After a few more short books, story time came to an end.

"Who wants a sticker?" the cowboy asked.

A chorus of "me's" rang out. D scrambled onto Virge's lap and hid his head against his chest, clutching Boo Bear tight. Running his hand down his little back and murmuring soothing sounds, he closed his eyes and tried to project calm to his nephew's small, trembling body.

"Hey, little partner. I saved a special sticker just for you."

D whipped around, and Virge opened his eyes. The cowboy had crouched down on one knee about two feet from them. Amazing, he managed that position without spearing himself in the ass with a spur. Even more amazing? His gorgeous face: steel-blue eyes, full pink lips, a sexy cleft in his chin, and a strong jaw covered with dark-blond stubble. A bump on his nose, indicating it had been broken in the past, only added to his masculine beauty. Small gold hoops adorned the cowboy's ears. Virge's dick, which had been hibernating for months, hardened. He shifted D in his lap. *Awkward.*

The cowboy smiled, a flash of perfect white teeth, and slowly held out a large marshal's star sticker. D snatched it up before signing "thank you." The man's eyes widened, and his smile went from gentle to megawatt as he signed back "you're welcome." The cowboy met his gaze and tipped his hat before rising with an easy grace he envied.

D gave the sticker to Virge and thrust his chest out to receive his prize. After placing the sticker on the little boy's shirt, he helped his nephew stand to the side then rose with a groan using knees not as young and nimble as the handsome cowboy's, and his ass went from numb to pins and needles. After a quick look around, he sighed with relief that the younger man had left before witnessing his less than dignified maneuver.

Chapter Two

The sexy cowboy remained on Virge's mind over the next few days. Sure, lots of attractive men lived in L.A., but the genuine warmth in those blue eyes stayed with him. Seemed the man had made an impression on his nephew, too.

"D, who is this?" Dr. Sarah asked, viewing his drawing.

The little boy turned to him, and Virge nodded encouragement. "Cowboy," D whispered.

Success! He smiled. Slowly but surely, his nephew was talking again.

He'd gone mute following Teisha's death. After months of no progress, the doctors had recommended Dr. Sarah Albright, one of the best child psychologists in the country, specializing in trauma and loss. He had immediately known she was a good fit. Professional, keenly observant, coupled with a gentle manner, Dr. Sarah had quickly gained D's trust.

"Very good!" The therapist's eyes lit up.

"A cowboy read to the kids at the library the other day," Virge added.

"Oh, yes, the Reading Wrangler. How fun."

D tapped his fingertips together in the "more" sign and squirmed in his chair. The excitement on his face warmed Virge with hope.

"He'll be back next week," Dr. Sarah said.

The little boy's face scrunched up, and tears filled his eyes. Logically, he knew his nephew had mercurial moods like any kid his age, but those tears tore at Virge's heart.

"Let me see what I can do." Dr. Sarah picked up her phone and dialed. "Hi, Sam. I've got a special little friend who's a fan of Nate's. Any chance he can visit the ranch?"

She listened before turning to him. "Tomorrow at ten work for you?"

"Sure."

"Great. Thanks, Sam." Dr. Sarah ended the call.

She provided directions to the ranch. He picked up D, who'd stopped crying once he knew he'd be seeing the cowboy again. "Thanks. I know he'll love to visit."

Dr. Sarah chuckled dryly. "Nathan Malone, the Pied Piper of children and women everywhere."

Hot disappointment slid through him, the severity taking him by surprise. Well, hell, this was rural Montana. Of course the hunk of a cowboy played for the other team. Yet he couldn't shake the pit at the bottom of his gut.

***

"Hey, you're looking better," Jared said, entering

Nate's room. His brother lay sprawled out on his bed, thumbing through a magazine.

"Yeah, I'm good now. I'd have done chores this evening, but Gabi recommended I take it easy until tomorrow." Their sister-in-law had attended medical school before leaving to fulfill her true dream of becoming a chef.

"Cool."

Nate set the magazine down. "Say, how did it go at the library the other day?"

"Good. The kids were really well-behaved. I wouldn't want to do it all the time, but I had fun."

"They're great and so curious. Like little knowledge sponges."

Nate continued to talk, but Jared's thoughts slipped to the handsome stranger from the library. Man, he was fine. Like smoking-hot, holy damn fine. Jared had stumbled while reading a few times, conscious of the handsome man's focus. His rich-mocha skin complemented his intense brown eyes, high cheekbones, strong square jaw, and lips made for kissing. Diamond studs winked from his ears. Where jeans ruled, the man wore slacks and a lavender button-down shirt rolled up to his elbows, showcasing strong forearms.

Jared had a thing for older men as they tended to be comfortable in their own skin. This man radiated confidence and was so gentle and protective of his cute little boy. Qualities Jared found extremely attractive. He frowned. The kid meant he was probably straight and married. He shook his head to erase the image of the gorgeous guy. He didn't need to court any trouble. Shit, that's why he hated going into town. Better to stay here on the ranch.

He rubbed his hands together. "I declare a *Call of Duty* marathon. Ready to get your ass kicked?"

"As if. Prepare to be massacred," Nate retorted.

Jared settled on the floor next to his brother's bed and grabbed a controller.

Chapter Three

Virge stifled a yawn and took a swig of coffee. D had awakened at five-thirty a.m., raring to go. They'd read and played together for hours. After breakfast, he convinced his nephew to play with his toys while he sat nearby to make a phone call.

"How's D?" his mom asked.

"He spoke another word to Dr. Sarah yesterday."

"Oh, that's fabulous! I miss you both. I wish I could be there."

"I know, but Auntie Ruth needs you, and I've got this covered."

"True. The doctors say she's recovering nicely. I have to remind her to take her medication though. I'm so proud of you stepping up for our little boy."

"I just did what needed to be done."

"Virge...."

"It's fine, really."

His mother sighed. "So, are the cowboys in Montana as cute as those boys from *Brokeback Mountain*?"

"Mom!"

"What? Inquiring minds want to know."

He pictured the handsome, straight Nathan Malone. "Yes, some of them are."

"Oh, good. Now you remember to have some fun."

"Mom...."

"I mean it. Teisha wouldn't want you to give up your happiness."

"My first priority is D." His nephew looked up, hearing his name. "Want to talk to Grammy?" Virge gave him the phone, and, not surprisingly, D didn't say anything but listened closely. The little boy waved at the phone and handed it back to him.

"He waved good-bye to you."

"Hope D likes the ranch. Call me when you get home. I want to hear all about it."

"Love you, Mom."

"Love you, too."

He pocketed his phone before grabbing the diaper bag. "Let's go, little man."

Virge flipped through the radio stations when they left town. He shuddered at the multitude of country music selections he came across and switched to D's current favorite CD, the *Frozen* soundtrack.

There was little traffic on the freeway. He tapped his fingers on the steering wheel and peered at D in the rearview mirror. The small boy stared out the window, but soon his eyes drifted closed. Virge smiled. The rhythmic motion of the vehicle almost guaranteed D would take a catnap during their forty-five-minute trip.

Following Dr. Sarah's directions, he slowed and turned onto the gravel road leading to the ranch. Good thing he'd purchased an SUV. His classic Corvette Stingray wasn't practical or safe for transporting a small child. It certainly wouldn't have done well on the roads here, either. Damn, he missed that car, spending weekends working on it with his dad when he was still alive. It'd felt like he'd lost him all over again when Virge sold "her." *You had to let go sometime.*

He pushed his thoughts aside as he drove under an arched sign. *Blackbird Ranch.* D stirred and yawned.

"Almost there, bud."

The ranch lay in a valley nestled among majestic mountains. The fabulous view belonged on a postcard. He'd never seen so much green and so much...nature. He couldn't take it all in.

Virge parked next to a few large pickup trucks and got out. He breathed in the incredible fresh air, still acclimating to its thinness. He helped his nephew out of his car seat and set him next to the SUV while a cowboy in familiar gear approached. D clapped his hands.

Nate Malone crouched in front of him. "Hey, buddy."

D gave an anguished cry and wrapped his arms around Virge's leg, mashing his face against it.

He understood the little guy's misery. While the man bore a strong resemblance, this was not their cowboy. The blond hair flowed almost to his shoulders, and the steel-blue eyes glittered with mischief instead of glowed with warmth.

The man shrugged and stood. "Gee, sorry about that. Normally, I'm really good with kids."

"Not your fault. He was just expecting someone else."

The cowboy frowned and then snapped his fingers. "You must mean my brother. He filled in for me the other day. You can meet him on the tour. Oh, I'm Nate by the way."

The hot cowboy is Nate's brother. Something suspiciously like hope filled him.

"I'm Virge, and this is D."

"Cool. Follow me." Nate turned and sauntered off.

His nephew released the death grip on his leg and raised his arms, signaling he wanted to be carried. Virge lifted him and caught up with the other man. Nate explained that Blackbird functioned as both a cattle and guest ranch. He pointed out the various guest buildings and the stables before approaching a riding arena.

Another blond cowboy stood in the middle, working with a horse. He had a long rope around its neck, guiding it around the ring at a quick clip. The shirtless cowboy spoke in a firm yet quiet tone. Virge nearly choked on his tongue, eyeing the golden skin and muscles on display. *This* was their cowboy.

The man whistled, and the horse stopped. He rubbed its shoulder, his back to them, as they reached the ring's split-rail fence.

"Daddy!" D shrieked, and the horse whinnied and shied, bumping into the man as it swung around.

"Whoa, easy, Spike," the cowboy soothed.

Virge struggled to prevent his nephew from launching out of his arms while the cowboy calmed the large, skittish animal. He'd never been near a horse and was struck by its size and power, which the other man skillfully controlled. As the cowboy turned, Virge saw a tattoo on his chest. A redwing blackbird with a rainbow-hued ribbon dangling from its beak. His heart beat a little faster seeing the colorful ink. Could he be gay? The cowboy handed the rope to a dark-haired man before pulling on a T-shirt that stretched tight over those muscles. He suppressed a disappointed sigh.

Nate chuckled. "You've got some explaining to do, bro."

"Hi, I'm Jared. I remember you from the library." He approached with a rolling gait Virge found sexy as fuck and offered his hand after wiping it against his denim-clad thigh. Damn, he was built all over and tall, just an inch or two shorter than his own height.

Virge shook his hand, hyperaware of the firm grasp of warm, work-hardened skin. "I'm Virge, and this is Donovan. He goes by D."

"Glad you could make it out—"

"Why did he call Jared daddy?" Nate interrupted.

"He calls all men daddy and women mommy. If he especially likes someone, he adds their first names. D doesn't talk much, so he must like Jared." What about this cowboy had inspired his nephew to talk?

"Oh, that's cool." Nate frowned and scuffed the dirt with the toe of a boot. "Why don't we check out the horses?"

D clapped and squirmed to be put down. He held onto Virge's hand while they walked into the stables with the brothers.

They toured the buildings and met the brothers' favorite horses. Nate took D to see his horse a few stalls down while Virge stayed with Jared.

"This is my horse, Angel." Jared stroked the neck of a beautiful black horse.

"You must be a Buffy fan," he said, and received a blank expression. *Shit, how old is he? Did he even get the reference?* "You know Spike and Angel from *Buffy the Vampire Slayer* and *Angel....*"

"Yeah, great shows, but Angel here's a girl."

"Oh, I thought all macho cowboys rode stallions."

Nate snorted. "City slicker."

"Stallions don't make good cattle horses. Too temperamental. All they think about is eating and you know...." Jared pumped his fist in the air to signify sex. Virge's mouth went dry as his mind immediately connected the handsome man with hot, sweaty sex.

Jared continued, "Distractions are dangerous. Man and horse have to be a team, or one or both will get injured, so we ride geldings or mares."

But do cowboys find sex a good distraction?

"Um, Virge, little dude is either working on the solution to ending world hunger, or he's going poopy," Nate said in a panicky voice.

D had only needed pull-ups at night, but, after Teisha died, he refused to use the toilet, making diapers a necessity. All the doctors said regression after a traumatic event was normal, and his nephew would become interested in returning to his big-boy ways when he was ready. Virge *really* looked forward to that day.

"May we use your bathroom?"

"Sure, just come up to the big house." Jared led them out of the stables.

"I need to grab the diaper bag." He stopped at the Subaru, unlocking it with a click of the fob.

The brothers chuckled and told him to come on inside. They left to join another tall, blond cowboy entering the house. This one easily topped his own six foot four by a few inches and was built like a mountain. "How many of them are there?" Virge muttered.

"Five, but that one is mine."

He turned and instantly recognized the handsome Latino. *Master R.* Virge had never expected to see the Dom here of all places. Their paths had crossed five years ago at an L.A. BDSM club while he did research for *Death in the Dungeon.*

"Are you here on vacation?" Virge asked.

"I live here. Married, actually."

"Marriage looks good on you." While Master R had masked it well, Virge remembered the bleakness that'd crept into his eyes and features during their discussions regarding BDSM relationships. He'd wondered what had caused the Dom such pain but refrained from asking.

The Dom smiled broadly. "Thank you. I heard about the movie deal. Congratulations."

"I wouldn't accept until they added the provision to hire your friend as a consultant on the first film."

Master R nodded. "He told me. Good to see our trust continues to be well-placed. We appreciated how you portrayed the community in the book."

"Your assistance was very helpful." While kink didn't do it for him, he'd come to respect what it meant to those who lived the lifestyle. That was why he researched everything. He wasn't about to fuck things up by not being thorough. That didn't work as a cop or a writer.

"What should I call you?" He figured the BDSM honorific wouldn't fly here.

"Rafael."

"I'm Virge," he supplied since he'd used his pen name at the club.

They shared a look, silently communicating their mutual understanding to protect each other's alternate identities.

D grumbled, and Virge slung the diaper bag over his shoulder, following Rafael into the house.

After dealing with the diaper and washing up, he and D emerged from the bathroom. He pulled them to a halt in the hallway while a short woman with long curly hair kissed yet another large, blond cowboy before handing over a sleeping baby bundled in a purple blanket. The man carried the infant past them with a hushed "hello."

Five of them. Damn.

"Hi, I'm Gabi." He shook her small hand and introduced them. Her shirt read, *The Sass is Strong with this One.* She had big brown eyes and a large smile. Even though she had shadows under her eyes, she had that new mom glow. A punch of sadness hit him hard. Just like Teisha during D's first few months.

His nephew made a rocking motion with his arms.

"Yes, Olivia's my baby girl," Gabi said.

Forcefully pushing down the gloom, he grinned. "I pity any boy who tries to date her, what with her daddy and four big uncles."

Rafael strode up and wrapped an arm around Gabi's shoulders. "And one very protective godfather."

Gabi giggled. "This is my cousin, Rafael."

"Yes, we met outside."

Gabi pointed to D's blue stuffed animal. "Who is this?"

D hid his face against Virge's leg, so he responded for him. "That's Boo Bear."

She grinned. "Great name. How old are you, D?"

His nephew held up three fingers.

"Three! Wow, what a big kid you are."

Virge had clocked enough time around preschoolers to know including half years was really important, so he added, "Three and a half."

D nodded and smiled.

Gabi grinned. "Lunch is just about ready. Please join us."

"Oh, I don't want to put you out."

D tugged Virge's pant leg and gave him a pleading look. Where had his timid nephew gone?

"Of course not. I've made a large batch of spaghetti so there's plenty to share. Any food allergies?"

"None. Thank you for including us."

She led them into a huge, open kitchen. His mom would be in heaven here. Gabi pulled garlic bread out of the oven while they lingered by the breakfast nook. His stomach rumbled. Damn, the bread and the simmering marinara sauce smelled delicious.

Jared and Nate joined them. Thankfully, Nate had ditched his Reading Wrangler outfit. "Something smells good, *mamacita*. I'm *dying* of hunger," he said.

Gabi chuckled. "Can't have you wasting away. Why don't you find a booster seat for D?"

His nephew raced over and latched onto Jared's leg like a crazed starfish. Virge smothered a grin at the cowboy's stunned expression and moved to rescue him.

"Jared, what do you have attached to your leg," Nate asked in fake horror.

His brother stared at him, his features furrowed in confusion.

Nate nudged his arm with his shoulder and prompted, "Looks like a dangerous beast. Could it be...?"

Jared's features cleared. "Oh, no. I have a puma on my leg. A puma on my leg." He walked around the room, dragging the leg D clung to. The little boy giggled and dropped Boo Bear to hold on tighter.

"How do I get him off? He's got me good."

Nate tapped his chin. "Hmmm, I hear they're mighty ticklish."

Jared stopped. "Is that right? How about I tickle the dangerous mountain lion," he said, wiggling his fingers a few inches from the little boy's sides.

"Daddy," D squealed and let go, falling back onto his butt.

The tall cowboy reached down and helped him up with a grin. "My name's Jared."

D smiled. "Daddy Ar-hed."

"Ha ha, he called you an airhead," Nate crowed, and the grin slipped off his brother's face.

Just when he started to warm to Nate, the man did something that made Virge want to bitch slap him. He pressed closer so only Jared could hear.

"When he tries to say Virgil it comes out gerbil."

Jared chuckled, a smile tugging at the corner of his mouth. Now that was what he liked to see.

With Gabi's prompting, everyone gathered in the dining room. He usually towered over almost everyone, so being with several people around the same height was disconcerting. It also made Gabi, at only a few inches over five feet, downright tiny compared to all the men. Rafael introduced his husband Wyatt and Sam, Gabi's spouse, as Virge settled D into a booster seat next to Jared. He counted four brothers and wondered about the fifth. Rafael must have noticed him looking around because he explained the youngest, Brett, was doing a veterinary internship in Washington state.

Gabi had cut D's noodles into short, manageable strands. The little boy frowned at the steamed carrots slices touching the spaghetti. Virge quickly moved them apart on the plate. Relieved his nephew began eating without a fuss, he tried to focus on his lunch and monitoring D rather than on Jared.

He asked about the ranch and was impressed with how each family member lent their skills to run it. Wyatt ran the cattle operation while Jared and Nate managed the guest business. Sam oversaw the finances. Even Brett planned to return and serve as the area's veterinarian.

"Where are you from, Virge?" Wyatt said.

"Born and raised in Los Angeles."

"Oh, have you met anyone famous?" Nate leaned forward in his chair.

"Sure, I've met a few." He shrugged. When they urged him to tell them who, he mentioned a couple. "Most of them are just like normal people."

"What do you do?" Gabi asked.

"I'm a homicide detective with the LAPD." That prompted some questions about the accuracy of TV cop shows.

"How long have you been in Montana?" Jared asked.

"Almost three weeks. I'm renting a furnished apartment on a monthly basis in Erwin."

Wyatt nodded. "Oh, yeah. The apartments off Fern Grove Drive. We've had a few seasonal ranch hands stay there. Heard it's decent."

"This must be really different from what you're used to," Nate said.

Understatement of the year, but he had no regrets. D's progress with Dr. Sarah gave Virge more hope than he'd had in months. "All these open spaces are an adjustment." And so quiet. He hadn't been able to sleep the first two nights because of it.

He glanced at D pushing his food around. "Please eat your carrots."

His nephew ignored him.

"Hey, little buddy. Did you know that carrots are really good for your eyes? And they taste pretty good, too. Want me to try first?"

D held one up, and Jared carefully extracted the slice from his grubby fingers before placing it into his mouth. Virge had to give the man props for not getting grossed out. The cowboy made a happy humming sound as he chewed. D turned back to his own plate and ate all the remaining carrots.

"How did you do that?" He couldn't contain his shock, staring at Jared over his nephew's head. The other man winked.

"I'm a reformed picky eater."

Laughter rumbled around the table.

Jared's cheeks flushed. "Well, mostly reformed."

Nate snorted. "Jared hates tomatoes but loves ketchup. He covers everything in it. Maybe he should marry it." He made kissy sounds and then laughed like a jackass.

Virge glared at Nate, who appeared oblivious to his irritation, but as he looked away his gaze collided with Rafael's. The Dom arched one elegant brow. *Busted.* Rafael's eyes widened as D growled fiercely. The little boy flung a handful of spaghetti across the table. It nailed Nate's cheek with a loud splat and slid down his face. The man's mouth gaped. Sputtering coughs masking laughter filled the room.

"Donovan Lance Stevens. That was not nice. Please apologize." Virge touched the boy's arm and received the full weight of his death glare. Damn, D had already mastered the family "don't fuck with me" expression. Maybe he'd become a cop like the last three generations of Stevens men.

Jared tapped D's other arm, and his nephew swung around to the cowboy. "My brother likes to poke fun, but he loves me and always has my back. Don't you, Nate?"

Nate paused from wiping his face and smiled broadly. "Sure do, bro." His eyes brightened. "Remember that time we got totally wasted—"

"Nate," Wyatt said in a quiet, yet authoritative tone.

Nate glanced at D. "Oops. So yeah, I shouldn't have picked on him, but I love Jared. All my brothers. Sorry, little man."

His nephew signed. "Sorry."

He accepted a damp washcloth from Gabi and

cleaned his nephew's face and hands.

"Thank you for lunch. We should probably hit the road."

"But you haven't had dessert yet. D, would you like to have a cookie and read some stories with me?" Gabi said.

The little boy nodded and held her hand as they left the dining room.

Jared and Sam brought in bowls of peach cobbler with vanilla ice cream. Virge dug in. *Delicious.* He idly wondered if there was a gym in town. He had already gained some weight while on leave. These guys must really work hard since they didn't appear to have an ounce of fat on them. He glanced around the table and noticed Nate still had some marinara sauce on his face. "You missed a spot," he said, pointing a finger to his own face indicating where.

The man chuckled as he wiped the sauce away with a napkin. "Schooled by a little kid. I'm never gonna live that down, am I?"

"Nope" and "no way" echoed around the table.

"I apologize for D's behavior. He lost his mother recently."

Rafael and the brothers gave their condolences.

"He's seeing Dr. Sarah," Sam said.

He nodded. "For selective mutism and PTSD. My captain granted me an extended leave so we could come here." A lump formed in his throat as he remembered how vibrant and outgoing D had been before Teisha died. God, he missed hearing his nephew's happy chatter.

"She's the best. Most of us saw her after our parents died in a plane crash," Jared said.

Sympathy swelled through him. "Were you all kids at the time?"

"Wyatt and I were in college. Jared and Nate were teenagers, and Brett was ten," Sam explained.

"That must have been very difficult."

"We had each other. D's lucky. It's clear you're a good father," Wyatt said.

"I'm actually his uncle. His dad passed away before he was born." He frowned. Lance would have been a great dad. He hadn't known Teisha was pregnant when he died. Virge had never decided if that made it better or worse.

"Shit, that fucking sucks huge, hairy donkey balls," Nate exclaimed.

"Little ears, Nate," Gabi called from the other room, and Sam smacked him upside the head.

"Your mouth has been running all morning. I'm thinking you need some time to reflect," Wyatt said.

Nate groaned. "Fine. I'll do dishes for a week."

"You were rude in front of our guests," Rafael added with a quelling expression.

"And I'll vacuum for a month." Nate grimaced.

Virge grinned. *You can take the Dom out of the dungeon, but you can't take the Dom out of the man.*

After everyone had finished eating, he excused himself and went to the family room. Surprisingly, Jared joined him instead of leaving with his brothers. His nephew snuggled close to Gabi on the couch, playing with her hair as she read to him. A black and white dog slept, curled up at her feet. Virge's heart lurched at how content the little boy appeared. Would he ever be able to give him everything he needed? Gabi finished the story, and she hugged D.

"What do you say to Gabi?"

D signed "thank you."

"Oh, he blew me a kiss. How sweet!" She returned the gesture.

"Actually, he signed 'thank you,'" Jared explained. "Where did he learn that?"

"His daycare teaches babies and toddlers some simple signs. It helps them communicate when they aren't verbal yet."

"I've heard of this. It would be great for Olivia," Gabi said. "Jared, will you teach me?"

"Sure." The cowboy shrugged.

His sexy, yet humble vibe pushed all of Virge's buttons. "I meant to ask you. Where did you learn to sign?"

A shadow passed over the other man's face. "I grew up with someone who's deaf."

D patted the dog while Virge thanked Gabi for a wonderful lunch. After slinging the diaper bag over his shoulder, he hefted D up and carried him outside.

Jared followed them out to the Subaru and waited while Virge placed D in his car seat.

"Let me give you my number. You're welcome to visit any time," Jared said.

He handed over his phone, and the cowboy quickly added his contact info before returning it.

"Thank you. I really appreciate you and your family taking time for us." Virge held out his hand for a shake.

Jared grasped it and pulled him into a bro hug. Damn if it didn't feel good. He couldn't remember the last time he'd been in a man's arms. Too damn long. The cowboy smelled amazing, a heady mix of leather, soap, and man.

They parted, and Jared stepped back as Virge got

into the SUV. With a final wave, the other man strode away.

Virge smiled. *Definitely looking forward to seeing him again soon.*

Chapter Four

Jared's thoughts strayed back to Virge. He'd looked fucking fantastic in a T-shirt and jeans. Drawn to his quiet strength, Jared had liked how Virge had rolled with his big, crazy family, and how he cared for his nephew. But the man had baggage and was a cop. After Blake, he couldn't do that again.

Forget about it. He's probably straight anyway.

Jared filled two large bowls of popcorn and carried them into the family room. He handed one to Nate before taking his spot on the couch.

"Those guys should just get over themselves and kiss."

Are we watching the same movie? "What? They hate each other. Besides they're straight."

"Nope, that's pure sexual tension. I'm totally shipping those two," Nate said confidently.

"Shipping?"

His brother looked at him incredulously. "You don't know what shipping is? You're gonna need to turn in your gay card."

"Pretty sure that's not how it works." Jared punched his arm.

Nate smirked. "Shipping is when fans pair characters into romantic relationships, straight or gay. Like Sherlock Holmes and Dr. Watson or Captain America and Iron Man. They even have celebrity couple nicknames like Johnlock or Stony."

"Steve Rogers and Tony Stark, like together-together?" *WTF? Does Wyatt know about this?*

"Sure. There's fan art and stories, too. Check this out. Gabi showed me this." Nate fiddled with his phone and held it up to display an image of Captain America and Iron Man up against a wall kissing. It was tastefully done but hot. *Make that super-hot.*

Nate chuckled. "Mind blown, right? And speaking of kissing, looked like you wanted to lay one on Virge big time."

Jared's mind stuttered at the swift topic change. "I did not." His cheeks burned.

"I saw you eye-fucking him and what you did before he left."

Jared shrugged. "It was just a hug. The guy looked like he needed one."

"Right.... And did you add the ranch's number into his phone or your personal digits? "

"Mine."

His brother stared at him.

"I'm sure he's straight, Nate."

"Your gaydar must be defective, bro, because he totally checked you out, too."

"Yeah?" Excitement spiked through him until reality returned. "Well, even if that was true, he's only here for a little while."

"So what? Live it up while he's here. Have some

fun. Have you been with anyone since Deputy Asshat?"

Jared sighed. "No."

"Dude, you broke up almost a year ago." Concern etched his brother's face.

"I know. Not like there's a lot of options around here." Jared shrugged a shoulder. And even if there had been, he doubted he would have gone looking. He'd needed time to regroup.

"All the more reason to get to know Mr. L.A. The man's total DILF material."

He sputtered out a laugh. *Lord, the things that come out of Nate's mouth.*

Nate's attention swung back to the TV. "I love this chase scene."

Thank God his brother had a squirrel brain and didn't bring Virge up again.

Instead of focusing on the movie, Jared thought about the possibility of dating. Could he truly be open with someone again after the emotional stomping he'd gotten from Blake? As his tension mounted, Jared rubbed his fingers over one thigh where his jeans covered the spider web of thin scars. Blake's last words echoed in his head. *No one else is gonna want you, Jared. You're damaged goods.*

He stood up. The abrupt movement got Nate's attention. "See you in the morning."

"You okay, bro?"

"I'm fine."

"You know I really am here for you, right?"

"I do. Thanks, Nate."

On his way upstairs, his phone rang. Peering at the screen, he grimaced. Unknown local call. He didn't answer. If it was someone legit, they could leave a voicemail, but it was probably Blake. Jared had blocked him, but it hadn't stopped the asshole from calling and texting from random numbers. Blake could go fuck himself. He refused to be the bit on the side.

Chapter Five

Virge jerked awake to D's screams. He stumbled out of bed and rushed to his nephew's room. His heart constricted as the little boy sobbed. Gathering his nephew up in his arms, he gently rocked him and hummed songs. Nightmares that had once been a nightly occurrence were less frequent. Even though Virge had weathered the aftermath of each, he'd never gotten used to them. No child should have to endure what D had. If he'd only been there....

He pushed the thought aside. He didn't have the time or energy to dredge up the past. Virge needed to focus on calming the little boy. He continued to rock him and talked about Blackbird Ranch. About the beautiful scenery, the horses, and their new friends. D relaxed, slumping against his chest.

"What would you like to do when we visit next time?" Virge asked.

"Ride horsie with Daddy Ar-hed," D whispered.

He rubbed his nephew's small back. "I bet we can make that happen."

D fell asleep, and Virge got him settled. He pulled a blanket over him and kissed his forehead before leaving the room.

He woke up for another round later that night, and they fell asleep in the recliner in the living room. He woke to his phone ringing. Groaning, he shifted in the chair so he could grab it off the side table. Damn, it was nine a.m. He rolled his head around, trying to work out a crick in his neck.

"Hi, Mom."

"Good morning, honey. I hope I didn't catch you at a bad time."

"No, it's fine. We have an appointment in an hour."

"How was the ranch? Sorry I missed your call. Auntie Ruth had a bad spell."

"Is she okay?" At ninety, his great-aunt was relatively healthy, but she'd recently fallen and sustained a concussion.

"She's feeling better now. I've asked her to move in with me permanently. She shouldn't be living on her own."

"Are you sure you can take that on? You have your own health issues to deal with. You know what your doctor says about stress."

"I'll be fine. Sandra and Jess will be stopping by regularly, too."

"That's good." Virge frowned, hating being too far away to help. At least his aunts were there.

"So what happened at the ranch?"

He told her about the visit, including the spaghetti incident.

"That little pistol!" She laughed. "They sound like really nice people."

"They are."

"D had a rough night last night." Somehow his mom always knew.

"Yeah. Don't know if all the activity or seeing Gabi and the little baby affected him. I'll talk to Dr. Sarah about it."

"All part of the healing process, I'm sure."

After ending the call, he got them ready to go to their session. Dr. Sarah was encouraged by D's experience with the Malone family, especially how verbal he'd been with Jared. Nightmares, while stressful, were his way of working through things. She agreed it would be beneficial for him to visit the ranch again.

They returned home, and while his nephew ate Cheerios and fruit, Virge texted Jared with a request to visit. The response back was quick and positive.

Sure. 4ish?

Great. Thanks.

Meet me in the stables.

See you then.

"D, we're going to the ranch this afternoon."

Despite his tired eyes, the little boy smiled brightly.

After lunch, D took a power nap. Virge had tried to catch some Z's as well but couldn't fully relax. The thought of seeing Jared soon had the same effect as a triple espresso. So instead, he'd grabbed his computer and studied the ranch's website, which led to searching the cowboy's social media presence. He discovered Jared was out and proud and fifteen years younger.

Damn, that's a big gap. His chest constricted as doubt filled him. Was he a fool for wanting the younger man's attention? Could he be setting himself up for rejection?

***

"Thanks for lending me your book, bro. It was frigging awesome. I totally didn't expect the twist at the end, and that Derek Price guy is something else. He's like James Bond and Luther's gay American love child," Nate said.

"Seriously, where do you come up with these things?"

Virge paused outside the stables with the surreal realization the brothers were talking about one of his books. Did he want to hear more? He'd avoided reading reviews after making the rookie mistake of googling his pen name years ago. Some of the comments had been pure vitriol. He stopped writing for months and had almost given up before Teisha's encouragement had finally gotten him back on track.

"I love the books, but Derek's like a machine. Nothing fazes him. If he showed some vulnerability, I could relate to him more," Jared said, a touch of wistfulness in his voice.

"Well, if I was gay, and he was real, I'd show him what a cowboy can do," Nate said with no small amount of swagger.

Jared laughed. "Derek's a total top. He'd chew you up and spit you out, little brother."

Virge smirked. *Hell yes, he would.*

He'd modeled Derek somewhat after himself and his experiences—only a hundred times more exciting. No one wanted to read about the mountains of paperwork actually required for each case or quiet nights watching TV. But had he gone too far? Virge turned Jared's words over in his mind as he carried D into the stables.

"Oh, hey guys," Nate greeted them. "Jared will get Angel saddled. Let's get a helmet for the little dude."

Virge followed him to the wall and helped select the right-sized helmet. Did he really want D doing something that required protective headgear?

Nate must have seen the doubt in his eyes. "He'll be totally safe, but we require all kids and beginners to wear helmets. Safety first."

They exited the stables and entered the riding arena. Jared soon joined them, leading Angel. Nate closed the gate behind him. Jared stopped next to them and whistled softly. His horse curtseyed. D laughed and clapped.

Jared slung himself onto the saddle and then reached down.

Virge lifted his nephew, a shiver running down his spine as his hands brushed Jared's. The cowboy settled D in front of him, one hand on him keeping him steady while holding the reins with the other. The little boy grasped the saddle horn and pumped his legs.

"Easy there, D," Jared said with a chuckle.

Nate beckoned Virge back against the fence, and Jared clicked at Angel who slowly rounded the arena. His nephew looked so tiny compared to the huge animal he rode with the large cowboy. He smiled at the little boy's giggles and gasps of excitement.

Nate grinned. "Kids are great."

Virge peered at the other man. "Is that why you do the library gig?"

"I got into some trouble as a teenager and did the job as part of my community service."

Nate a troublemaker, shocking. "What'd you do?"

"Took the sheriff's cruiser for a joy ride." Nate chuckled.

"Damn, how many hours did you receive? You should have been done years ago."

"I did the mandatory time in a few months but continued on until I went to college. No one else did it after I left, and I hated disappointing the kids so I picked it back up once I came home for good."

Realizing there was more to Nate than his cocky persona, Virge met his eyes. "You'll make a good dad someday."

The other man clenched his jaw hard enough to make a muscle twitch there before he gave a tight smile. "Doesn't look like that's in the cards for me." Nate stepped forward and said, "How about we show the little dude how to groom Angel next."

Virge wondered what nerve he'd inadvertently struck with Nate as he approached to receive his nephew from Jared.

"What do you say, D?" he prompted.

"Thank you, Daddy Ar-hed." He signed "thank you" as well.

"You're welcome, bud. How about you call me J?"

"Daddy J." The little boy beamed at the cowboy.

Jared smiled. "There you go."

They returned to the stables, and Jared stopped in the aisle. "We'll do this out here rather than in Angel's stall." He dismounted and removed the saddle and other equipment Virge didn't know the names of, handing them off to Nate.

Jared accepted a brush from his brother before picking D up and showing him how to groom Angel.

"A good cowboy takes care of his horse at all times," Jared explained to the little boy.

His nephew cooed at the horse, and she nuzzled him. Jared fished out a baby carrot from his pocket and showed D how to hold it with his hand flat.

As the big animal's mouth approached the tiny hand, Virge's heart shot into his throat, but Angel gently took it from him. His nephew giggled as the horse's velvety lips brushed his palm.

The brothers invited them into the house, where they found Gabi in the kitchen.

"D, would you like to help me make cookies?"

He nodded and looked at Virge.

"Sure, let's get you washed up first."

Once they returned, Gabi said, "Why don't you have some lemonade and sit on the porch for a while? Looks like you could use a break."

"Are you sure?" He wasn't used to leaving his nephew with anyone other than his mom.

She nodded. "D and I will have a great time."

"I'll help, too," Nate said, rubbing his hands together.

"Only if you don't eat all the cookies." Gabi gave him the side eye.

Jared poured him a lemonade, and he followed him out to the porch. They sat in chairs next to each other and gazed out over the land.

"D's a good kid. Nate usually works with the little ones who visit the ranch," Jared said before taking a sip of lemonade.

Bittersweet memories washed over him. "I've

been with him since the start. Took my sister to all the doctor's appointments and parenting classes, and my mom and I helped Teisha through labor. I even got to give him his first bath." Virge laughed. "I was more scared of holding his tiny little body than anything I've experienced on the force. I've been lucky enough to experience all his milestones."

"You mentioned his dad passed away."

"Yeah, car accident. Other driver was texting. Lance had just gotten home on leave from the Navy, and they planned to get married the following week."

Jared gave a low whistle. "Damn, that must have been really hard on your families."

"Damn hard, for sure, but I never met his family. They disowned him when he started dating Teisha."

The other man turned to glance at him. "Why?"

"They don't approve of interracial couples."

Jared shook his head. "That's awful. What about D?"

"They don't recognize him as their grandson." Virge frowned.

"That's messed up. How could they ignore such a sweet kid?" Jared scowled.

"I wondered the same thing. Our family helped my sister out as much as we could. We lost her four months ago." He paused to take a breath. "She took D to the park near their apartment. Some kids had a gun they'd found in their older brother's room. It went off, and Teisha was hit and died instantly. D clung to her, and they had trouble pulling him away from her body. They told me he screamed until he went hoarse. He stopped talking after that." A tear ran down Virge's cheek. "I wasn't there. I'd been out late at a crime scene the night before and overslept. If

I'd been there...."

"I know from experience that the 'what ifs' can eat you up. Don't blame yourself." A breathtakingly earnest expression filled Jared's face as he grasped his forearm, the simple touch lighting a match within only to be snuffed out when the other man released him. Virge mentally shook himself and returned to his story.

"Because I was listed in Teisha's will, I quickly received emergency guardianship. I now have full guardianship and am in the process of adopting him, but it takes time. Sometimes I worry I'm going to fuck things up."

"You'll do fine. Wyatt was only twenty-two when our parents died, but we all turned out okay."

Virge clucked his tongue. "Just a kid himself."

"Yep. Bob and Cookie helped out a lot, too."

"Your grandparents?"

"Former foreman and cook, but they're more family than employees. They live nearby but are currently on an RV trip around the country."

"That sounds like fun. Do you travel much?"

"Nah, everything I love is right here." Jared smiled at him, and Virge realized he had subconsciously leaned closer to the younger man. He went to move back until he saw Jared's eyes focus on his lips. He inched close enough to feel the other man's breath on his face.

"Who wants cookies?" Nate's voice had the same effect as being splashed with ice water.

They sprang away from each other.

Virge stood. "I should go see how D is doing."

"I need to check on the horses." Jared strode toward the stables.

Virge stared after him. He had no business getting involved with the younger man, but his body ached for him.

Chapter Six

Virge reminded D that Nate would be at the library instead of his brother. He didn't want a meltdown since Jared was still his nephew's favorite Malone. D settled in the last row of kids while he stood in the back with a few moms.

"What a cute little boy," they gushed, and he thanked them, a little uncomfortable interacting with other parents.

Nate held his young audience captive with goofy voices and sound effects as he read. While Jared was quiet and warm, his brother oozed fun and charisma. Nate reminded him of the actor Chris Pratt, only more obnoxious.

When story time ended and most of the kids had left, D skipped to the front. "Daddy Nate!" He raised his arms to be picked up.

For a brief moment, sadness flickered over the cowboy's face before he grinned and lifted the little boy, placing him on his knee.

"Now that's just between you and me. At the library, I'm called the Reading Wrangler. Don't blow my secret identity, little dude."

Virge didn't know if his nephew understood what Nate was saying, but he dutifully parroted "Reading Wrangler" which came out sounding more like "Eating Anger."

Nate chuckled. "D, you're totally awesome."

His nephew responded by holding up a small fist which Nate gently tapped with his own before moving his hand back, splaying his fingers wide, and exclaiming "Booyah!" with the little boy following along. The two grinned at each other.

He shook his head. The man had a quirky ability to put people at ease when he wasn't pissing them off.

Later that afternoon, he called home to check in. "D had a great day today. Since he's doing well at the library, Dr. Sarah wants him to try preschool starting for an hour and building up."

"But he's still in diapers," his mom said.

"Yeah, I brought that up, too, but she said they can make accommodations, especially with me there to assist, at least at first."

"That's exciting. When do you start?"

"Monday."

"How are you doing?"

"Good. Finally feeling settled here. I'm starting to feel like writing again."

"Wonderful. You going to add any hunkalious cowboys to this one? Derek could use some variety."

"Are you trying to make me blush?"

His mom chuckled. "We got Auntie Ruth all moved in. She seems happier now."

"That's great."

"Her birthday is coming up. Can you come visit?"

"Not sure. D's making such good progress, I'd

hate to mess with his routine."

"I understand. Our baby comes first."

"Give Auntie Ruth a hug for me."

Chapter Seven

Jared heard a vehicle drive up and ventured out of the stables. Frowning, he stalked over to the brown and white Bronco as Blake parked and got out. Fucker must have heard his brothers were gone.

"What are you doing here?" Jared placed his hands on his hips.

"Just stopped by to see you." Blake pursed his lips. "You're not answering my texts or calls."

"I've got nothing to say to you."

"Katie's at her mom's all weekend. You want to come over for pizza and watch a game?"

"I don't think so."

"God. Why do you have to make a big deal out of things? Stop being pissy and have some fun. It'll be like old times. Katie's a real bitch now that she's pregnant."

Jared scowled. "You need to leave."

"No." Blake grabbed him and slammed him roughly against the SUV, pinning him to the vehicle. Anger and a trace of fear coursed through him as

Blake smashed his lips with a kiss brutal enough for Jared to taste blood.

He jerked his head to the side and shoved him. "Back the fuck up. You've got no right. You're married, asshole," he growled.

Blake stumbled away a few steps and raised his hands in a placating manner.

"I didn't have a choice. I'm running for sheriff this fall. The voters expect a respectable family man," Blake said in a wheedling tone.

"You wouldn't know what respectable was if it smacked you in the face. Unless you have something official to discuss, Deputy Ashford, get the fuck off my land."

Blake glared and pointed a finger at him. "You'll regret this." He climbed into his SUV and slammed the door. A dust cloud followed the Bronco as it sped down the driveway.

Jared spat on the ground and wiped his mouth with the back of an unsteady hand. His lip stung like a bitch. He touched it gingerly. *Fuck.*

***

Virge slowed and moved farther to the right of the narrow road when a sheriff's vehicle drove up, gravel flying. The driver stared at him as he passed. Fuck, he hoped everything was okay at the ranch.

As he pulled up to the house, he saw Jared and Gabi on the porch. Gabi's large, angry hand gestures and Jared's grim expression indicated a heated discussion. Alerted to the approaching SUV, Jared assumed a poker face while Gabi scowled.

After parking and getting D, he walked up.

"Everything okay? I saw the cop," Virge kept his tone neutral.

"Fine. Just a social call," Jared bit out. "I need to get cleaned up, and then we can practice riding. Gabi, could you get them a drink?" The cowboy left without waiting for her response.

Gabi growled out a long string of very creative curse words in Spanish. He winced. Damn, the sweet lady had a potty mouth to rival some of the street punks he'd busted.

"Blake the snake," she muttered in English as she led them into the kitchen.

"Are you sure everything's okay?" He'd never seen her this riled up. D whimpered and clung to his jeans, likely picking up on her tension.

Seeming to remember their presence, she smiled or at least tried. The number of teeth bared was intimidating. "Sorry, yes. Just a little disagreement." The look she gave him told him to drop it. She handed them lemonade.

"Where is everyone?"

"Moving cattle to another pasture. They're out for a few days with guests. Jared drew the short straw to stay with Olivia and me."

"I get to sleep in my own bed and have Gabi feed me. I'll take the short straw any day," Jared said as he came into the kitchen.

"Normally, Sam would stay, but I begged Wyatt to take him. New daddy needs a break, and I need a break from new daddy, even though he doesn't realize it." A real smile met Gabi's lips this time.

"He's nervous," Virge guessed.

"I love the man to pieces, but he hovers like Olivia or I will break." Gabi groaned when her phone rang. "Next time, I'm taking his SAT phone away."

Jared and Virge chuckled. After D finished his drink, they went outside.

"Let me introduce you to a sweet old lady." Jared led them to the ring where a gray-and-white horse patiently waited. "D, this is Poppy. She was my mom's horse, and she's real gentle. Would you like to meet her?"

"Yes!" D cheered.

Jared lifted him so he could pet her. She made a contented little sound and blew gently into his face. The little boy giggled.

"I knew she'd like you." Jared strapped on D's helmet and placed him on the kid-sized saddle, showing him how to hold the reins.

Trust in Jared and concern for his nephew grappled for domination. "Isn't he too little to be on alone?"

"We were on horses before we could walk." The cowboy adjusted the stirrups.

"Yeah, but you have cowboy genetics. D's a city boy."

Virge chewed on the rough edge of a fingernail as Jared led the large animal around in a slow circle, his body pressed close to her side. The horse plodded along at turtle speed, but D looked so tiny and fragile. The little boy didn't share any of his apprehension. He beamed with a huge smile.

"He's a natural, and Miss Poppy is what we call blast proof," Jared said in a reassuring tone, likely the one reserved for nervous guests.

"What does that mean exactly?"

"No sounds or sudden movements make her startle."

As they continued to circle, his unease dissolved. He had no reason not to fully trust that the other man would keep D safe. And look at the little boy go. Pride swelled as he watched his nephew ride and then help Jared groom the horse.

"Thank you for working with him. I can tell it's helping," he said as they got ready to leave.

"It's no hardship. I like spending time with him." Jared peered at him, his eyes shadowed by his hat brim, and smiled. "And you."

Virge's pulse picked up. "Good. I'd hate to wear out our welcome."

"Don't see that happening." Jared bumped his shoulder with his own, and he fucking loved the contact.

Chapter Eight

Two weeks passed. D continued making remarkable progress and rarely had nightmares. Virge now stayed in the hall during his nephew's two hours of preschool, close by but no longer needed in the same room. With more consistent sleep, Virge finally felt human again and, for the first time in months, was writing.

It was like the floodgates had opened. Ideas and plot points popped into his head at odd times, and he kept a notebook around to capture them. He caught himself doing stupid things like trying to put the milk in the cupboard and the cereal in the fridge. He'd created a new character, a handsome vice detective who bore a striking resemblance to Jared. A man to drive Derek crazy and ultimately make him want things he'd never wanted before. Sexual tension poured onto the pages, fueled by his unmet need for Jared.

Their routine revolved around therapy, preschool, and visits to Blackbird. Even with chores to do and guests to entertain, the Malones carved out time for them. D received attention from each of the brothers as well as from Gabi and Rafael. The family also seemed to understand that Virge needed time with other adults. It kept him sane, and being around Jared made him feel alive. Simple touches and shared glances, the flares of heat that couldn't be acted upon while surrounded by others, had become prolonged foreplay.

Virge exited the grocery store, pushing D riding on a cart one day, when he spotted a deputy hovering near their SUV. The man wrote down the license plate. Virge recognized the brown-haired cop who'd paid Jared the "social visit." The deputy wore mirrored sunglasses, and his muscular form actually made the drab brown uniform look good. Ashford was printed on the name tag under his badge.

Virge slowly approached the Subaru and stopped several feet away. "Is there something I can help you with, sir?"

"You own this vehicle?"

D turned to see who had spoken. Virge patted his leg reassuringly.

"Yes, sir."

"American-made not good enough?" Ashford asked, one note off from a sneer.

Virge grunted. *What a dipshit.* "It was made in Lafayette, Indiana."

The deputy's eyebrows rose. "That a fact?"

"Yes." *And with love, asshole.*

"California plates. You're a long way from home." Ashford yanked off his sunglasses and stared at him, his eyes hard. "I've seen you hanging around the Malone ranch. What's your business there?"

And there it is. Blake the snake. Just as Gabi saw

him.

"My kid likes their horses."

Ashford ambled to the cart and peered down at D. Virge tensed, reminding himself to remain still and nonthreatening.

"Hey there, little guy. How are you doing?" Ashford said in the baby-talk tone most kids hated.

Virge suppressed a grin at his nephew's baleful stare.

The deputy frowned and started to say something, but his cell rang. "One second," he said, stepping away and answering his phone. "Ashford." He listened for a few seconds. "Yes. I'll follow up."

The deputy ended the call. "I've got a bit of advice for you."

"And what would that be?"

"Stay away from the Malones. They're good people. I'd hate to see them get hurt." Ashford yanked his sunglasses back on.

"Me, neither." Virge struggled not to snarl. He watched as the deputy strutted to his vehicle and waited until he left before loading their groceries into the Subaru.

Nate met them as they pulled up in front of the house. "Hope we're not too late. Got delayed. I've got a cooler full of beer and ice cream."

"Sweet."

"Do you know a Deputy Ashford? Caught him checking out my SUV in the grocery store parking lot."

"Deputy Dumbass? You have got to be kidding me. What did he do?"

"Warned me off. Seemed to think I was a threat to your family."

"He's in no position to protect us. We take care of our own. And that includes you and D. Let us know if he pulls something again," Nate growled.

"What's his problem?" he asked as he helped D from the SUV.

"Not my story to tell." Nate pursed his lips and frowned. Strange for a guy who never shut up. Virge decided not to press further.

Nate grabbed the cooler and turned to D. "Let's bring this inside, little man. It's just us bachelors tonight, but Gabi left us dinner. Virge, can you let Jared know it's time to eat? He's out back washing the ATVs."

Virge rounded the house. Jared was shirtless and wearing earbuds, dancing as he hosed down a vehicle. He froze, mesmerized by the shaking ass in tight jeans. Who knew country boys could work it?

"See something you like?" Jared said with a smirk, but the vulnerability in his eyes and tension in his shoulders belied the cocky expression.

This and meeting the "delightful" deputy, set him in motion. Jared shifted to fully face him, and Virge cupped his jaw. "I do."

Their eyes locked, and then Jared's glance dropped to his lips before licking his own. *Jesus.* Virge leaned in slowly, giving the other man time to retreat. Instead, Jared's eyes closed, and he sighed as their lips brushed. What started as a small reassurance raged into a full-scale kiss. Jared dropped the hose and wrapped his arms around Virge. He stroked the cowboy's back before grabbing two handfuls of his spectacular ass. The other man groaned and pressed closer, their tongues dancing. They jerked apart at the sound of clapping.

"Dudes, it's about time! I had blue balls just being around you."

"Play with blue balls?" D asked from behind him.

"Shit." Shock stamped Nate's face before he spun around to find his small shadow.

"Shit!" the little boy parroted.

Groaning, Nate held up a hand. "I know, I know. A month of dishes and two months of vacuuming. Come on, little man, before I get myself in any more trouble." Nate steered D toward the front of the house.

Virge rested his forehead against Jared's and chuckled. "I was supposed to be telling you about dinner, not mauling you."

"I fully participated, so I'm not sure it could be called a mauling. I'm only sorry my brother interrupted us."

"Yeah?"

"Mmhmm. Let's go eat." Jared turned off the water, and they joined the others, who had placed the food and plates along with milk for D and beer for the men on one of the picnic tables in the front yard.

Virge sat next to Jared, their knees often brushing. Jesus, just like he was sixteen again. They ate in relative silence, listening to Nate entertain D with a goofy story. His nephew ate most of his dinner before asking to play close by.

"I'll deny it if you tell my mom, but this fried chicken's even better than hers."

"Gabi's awesome. We're lucky she left her swanky chef job in New York," Jared said.

"You Malone men are a persuasive bunch." His cheeks heated, and he distanced himself from the hot cowboy, picking up a large tub of bubble solution and wands at his feet. He showed D how to use them and make different shapes before handing them over. Nate finished his dinner and joined the little boy, running around blowing and popping bubbles. Virge envied Nate's boundless energy.

"What was it like growing up here?" he asked Jared who straddled the bench to face him.

Jared spoke about the tiny school they'd attended and the adventures the Malone brothers had as kids. Virge couldn't remember the last time he'd laughed so much.

"What happened here?" He ran a finger down Jared's nose. The other man scrunched it up in response. *Adorable.*

"Jack Anderson. Big, mean son of a bitch. He'd flunked a few times so he was older than anyone else in our sophomore class. We shared the same bus stop because his daddy worked on the ranch next to ours.

One day, as soon as the bus dropped us off, he began yelling at me. Giving me shit for being gay. I ignored him and started walking home with Nate. Jack spun me around by my backpack and punched me in the face. I went down like a ton of bricks. Nate went after him like a wolverine on crack, scratching, kicking, you name it. Now you gotta picture, Nate was only thirteen, skinny as a stick, and all knees, elbows, and big feet. Jack finally pinned him, and Nate launched his other weapon—his mouth." Jared paused to grin. "He said 'My brother Wyatt's bigger than you. He could kick you and your daddy's asses all the way to Texas with one hand tied behind his back.' The guy didn't look one bit scared and said something about his daddy calling Wyatt a fairy and he wasn't afraid of no fairies. I started to crawl toward them, ready for Nate to get the beat down, but Jack didn't land one punch because Wyatt stood there looking about eight feet tall with hands the size of dinner plates. My brother didn't yell, which made him even scarier. He said something like 'You will leave my brothers alone, you hear?' Jack nodded frantically and took off. I'm pretty sure he pissed his pants."

"Did he ever bother you again?"

"Nope. He stayed clear of us, and, after a few months, he and his daddy moved away. With all my brothers, he was really the only one dumb enough to give me shit."

"I wish I'd had a larger family. I loved my sister but always wanted a brother."

Jared shrugged. "When I was a kid, it felt really crowded sometimes. Everyone had their roles. Wyatt was the boss, Sam the brain, Nate the wild child, and Brett the baby. Which left me smack damn in the middle. Didn't really know how I fit in." He chuckled. "Lord, I sound like Jan Brady. 'Marcia, Marcia, Marcia,'" he exclaimed, and dramatically flicked a hand through his short hair.

Virge grinned. "How do you even know about *The Brady Bunch*? I was pretty young when it aired."

"We saw the remake, and we watched reruns of the original show on late night. Nate thought Marcia was hot." Jared smirked.

"I totally did," Nate called out as he passed on all fours with D riding on his back.

"Oh, yeah. I forgot they'd done a remake. Do you know how you fit now?"

Jared shrugged again. "I'm just me."

Nate passed by from the other direction. "You're

glue!"

"Huh?" Jared turned to his brother. "You make no sense sometimes, Nate."

"You're the glue that holds this family together, idiot. It would be a complete disaster if you weren't here to help with the ranch, the guests, and keeping the peace between all of us. Lord just keeping me in line is a full-time job."

He smiled as Jared blushed. Who'd have thought a tough cowboy could have a shy side?

"Oh. Thank you, Nate."

"Don't let it go to your head, though. You still totally suck at *Call of Duty.*"

"Dude, that's harsh." Jared grimaced, but a smile tugged at his mouth.

"Just keepin' it real." Nate smirked.

D fell asleep soon after dessert. Virge secured him in his car seat while Jared waited.

"Good night, Virge," he said softly, leaning in to kiss his cheek.

He tried not to grin like an idiot. If the cowboy wanted to be sweet, sign him the fuck up. He stared into Jared's eyes and brushed his fingers along the other man's jaw. "Good night."

Chapter Nine

Virge hesitated calling Jared, not wanting to come off pushy or too needy, but D made it unavoidable.

"'Lo?" Jared's sleep-roughened voice hit him low in the gut.

"Sorry, did I wake you?' He glanced at his watch. Nine p.m.

"It's okay. I fell asleep on the couch watching a movie. What's up?"

"I can't find Boo Bear. D won't go to sleep without him. I've looked everywhere. Could you check around and see if you can find him?"

"Hold on."

He heard rustling and imagined Jared's long, hard body unfolding off the couch. It was strangely intimate listening as he moved from room to room reporting in a low voice as he went.

"Not in the kitchen." Jared stopped talking, and Virge heard a soft knock. "Sam, have you seen D's bear?"

Sam mumbled and then the brothers chuckled.

"Duke. Bad boy," Sam admonished.

"We found Boo in Duke's bed. Fool dog is snuggling him," Jared said.

"Great. I'll tell D. If he knows you have him, maybe he'll go to sleep." *Fat chance.*

"I can leave now and drop him off."

"It's a long drive, and you're tired."

"Nah, it's fine. I just had a power nap. Put D on."

His nephew listened and then said, "Thank you, Daddy J." He made a kissy sound before handing Virge the phone. *Damn, that was cute.*

After giving Jared the apartment number, he disconnected. He put on a video to keep D calm while he straightened up, making sure to hide all his author stuff. Good thing he got right to it because Jared soon arrived. He must have hauled ass because the trip took Virge nearly double the time.

He let the cowboy in, trying not to be obvious as he checked out his rumpled appearance and sleepy expression. Jared's heavy-lidded blue eyes smoldered. Damn, he didn't have defenses for this level of sexy.

"Daddy J!" D rushed over and clutched Jared's leg before accepting Boo. He hugged the stuffed toy tightly and kissed its oversized head. Virge winced, thinking about dog germs.

"I found something in my desk drawer I thought you'd like, too." Jared pulled a Matchbox car from his front jeans pocket and gave it to D.

The little boy's eyes went wide, and he smiled.

Jared shot a semi-panicked look at Virge. "Is it age appropriate? Shoot, I should have asked before giving it to him."

"They're meant for older kids, but he doesn't put

stuff in his mouth so he has a few of these. Mainly have to make sure the wheels aren't loose. D, let me see."

"Daddy Vir, it's Lou," his nephew exclaimed, placing it in his hand.

He studied the black Corvette, checking the wheels before returning it. "You're right. Just like Lucy."

"Lucy?"

"My Vette."

"Really? I've always wanted to drive one. Do you have a picture?"

Virge had taken several when he put her up for sale. He located them on his phone and passed it to Jared who whistled appreciatively as he swiped through the photos. "What a beaut. A '69?"

"Yep. She's found a new home."

"That's a damn shame." Jared returned the phone.

He grinned. Teisha had always called Lucy a stud magnet. Seemed she worked her magic on hunky cowboys, too. He pictured driving along the California coastline with Jared at his side. That would have been nice.

"Thank you for coming all the way out to return Boo. Can I get you a drink while I get D settled?"

The cowboy opened his mouth, but before he said anything, D grabbed his hand and tugged. "Read."

"Jared doesn't—"

"No, it's okay. Lead the way, little man."

His nephew gave him a book and crawled into bed. The man sat in the chair by the bed and began to read.

The small boy shook his head. "No. Hands, too."

Virge grimaced. "D, you're being a bossy little mister."

"Please, please, please," his nephew pleaded, throwing in the "more" sign for good measure.

Jared chuckled. "Virge, take the book, and we'll switch places." Once they'd moved, the cowboy read and signed along. Soon, the little boy's eyes drooped, and he was asleep by the end of the story.

He kissed his nephew's forehead before turning off the light and closing the door most of the way. They returned to the living room.

"Thanks for humoring him. He should be out for hours."

"No problem. Well, I'd better head home."

Virge followed him to the front door where they both stopped, sexual heat sparking between them. He crowded into Jared's space and kissed him as if they hadn't seen each other in weeks. He accidentally knocked Jared's hat to the floor, and the cowboy groaned and wrapped his arms around his waist. His heart pounded. The other man placed a hand on his chest, pushing slightly. Virge released his mouth and met his eyes.

"Do you have a man waiting for you in L.A.?"

He palmed Jared's stubbled cheek. "I wouldn't be kissing you if I did."

"Good." The cowboy rewarded him with soft, tender kisses before nuzzling against his neck. Do you know what?"

His brain shorted out from the cowboy's touch, and it took him a few seconds to respond. "What?"

"I kept thinking about kissing you after you left."

"Was that the only thing you've thought about?"

Virge cupped his firm butt and squeezed. Jesus, the man's ass was perfection.

"Nope, I have a very vivid imagination." Jared dropped to his knees, pulling Virge's shorts and briefs down in one motion as he went. He groaned softly and braced a hand on the door as Jared licked his dick before engulfing it in his hot mouth.

Virge stared down at the beautiful man sucking him stupid. He slid his free hand through the golden-blond hair. It was so soft. Jared moaned, and Virge stroked his head in encouragement.

Jared took him deep, and he groaned as he felt his throat close around him. So fucking good. He was going to come. Virge tried to pull away, tugging at Jared's hair.

"I'm going to...."

The other man made a growly sound and grasped the back of his thighs, holding him tight.

With a low cry, he came, shooting into the cowboy's mouth. Jared licked him before rising. Virge pulled him close for a kiss, tasting himself on the other man's tongue. Reaching between them, he palmed Jared's erection, stroking the denim covering it. Jared groaned into his mouth. *So hot.*

"Let me take care of you." He fumbled with the other man's jeans button, giving a grunt of satisfaction when it came undone.

Jared flinched as if he'd been electrocuted. "It's getting late. I should go."

Virge dropped his hands. "What...?"

"See you later." Jared's face was unreadable as he stooped to pick up his hat before leaving.

Virge sagged against the closed door and took a shaky breath. His body still simmered with pleasure, while his mind raced in confusion. What had he done wrong?

Chapter Ten

J ared hadn't expected Nate to be awake when he got home. Instead of being dead to the world, his brother was brushing his teeth. For all his carefree tendencies, Nate had always been oddly meticulous about dental hygiene.

Nate spat into the sink. "Messed up hair and swollen lips. Looks like you delivered more than teddy bears," he said with a smirk which quickly turned into a concerned expression. "You're freaking out. What's wrong?"

Jared grimaced. "I fucked up."

"Come talk to Papa Nate."

Jared snorted but followed Nate into his bedroom which looked like it'd been hit by a tornado. *Papa Nate.* Jared had spent the majority of his life getting him out of scrapes. He was really screwed if he needed advice from his little bro. He sat on the edge of the unmade bed, while his brother sprawled.

"What happened?"

Jared flushed. Damn, this was embarrassing.

"Hey, you can tell me anything. I won't tell a

soul, cross my heart. I've got your back, bro."

Rather than start off with his epic screwup, he began at the beginning to build up his courage. "So I returned D's bear. He asked me to read a story, which I did. He fell asleep, and I went to leave, but Virge and I started kissing. It got hot pretty fast and...I blew him." The last part came out barely above a whisper. He bit his lip.

"So what went wrong? He get rough with you? I'll kick his ass if he hurt you." Nate scowled and cracked his knuckles.

"No, it was fine. Real good. We started kissing again, and he unbuttoned my jeans. I panicked and left." Jared groaned. "God, he must think I'm crazy. No one in his right mind would turn down a blow job from a sexy guy."

"So why did you?"

"I was afraid, afraid he'd see...." Jared nervously ran his fingertips over his thigh.

Nate's eyes followed the motion. "You didn't want him to see your scars?"

He nodded.

His brother let out a burst of air through pursed lips. "You were with guys in college, and it wasn't a big deal, right?"

Again Jared nodded.

Nate frowned. "Deputy Dipwad made you self-conscious, didn't he?"

"Yeah, he told me they were ugly. That I was damaged." His shoulders slumped as Blake's words echoed in his head.

"What an asshole. He's a fucking loser who didn't deserve you. You feel me?"

"I do, but a part of me wonders if Virge would

think the same."

"Well, if he did, he wouldn't be worth your time. But Virge has been around the block a few times, and I doubt they'd bother him. Wyatt has that really gnarly scar on his leg from when he tangled with barbed wire. Do you think Virge would care?"

"No, but that was an accident. He didn't do it to himself."

"You're not that person anymore. Yeah, it sucks you have physical reminders, but we all carry our mistakes around both on the inside and out." Nate's eyes darkened momentarily before he winked. "Like the Superman tat on my ass." He snapped his fingers. "I heard it's possible to tattoo over scars. If they really bother you, go check it out." Nate pulled him into a one-armed hug. "You're one of the strongest people I know. Don't let ancient history and a piece of shit ex get you down. It's not worth it."

"Thanks, Nate."

"You're welcome. Now get out of here. I need my beauty sleep."

Jared snorted. "Yes, princess."

Chapter Eleven

J ared glanced through the window of the tattoo parlor before entering the nearly empty shop.

A slender, dark-haired woman with tats and piercings glanced up from a magazine. "I'm Shanna. What can I do for you?"

"Hi, Shanna, I'm Jared. I don't have an appointment or anything, but I have a few questions."

"Sure."

"I read about tattoos covering scars. Is that something you can do here?"

"Depends on the size and depth. I can take a look and let you know what I can do. It would be free of charge."

Go for it. You've come this far. "Okay."

They went into the next room, and she indicated for him to sit in the chair. Jared hesitated. "They're on my thighs."

Shanna chuckled. "Go ahead and drop trou. Nothing you've got will mess with my female sensibilities." She perched on a stool with wheels.

Jared undid his pants and pulled them down before sitting on the chair. He fisted the bottoms of his boxer briefs and tugged them up towards his crotch.

She turned on a light with a long, adjustable neck and studied his skin. "On this side the scars are thin and shallow. Should be fairly easy to cover. Honestly, they're not very noticeable through the hair." She wheeled around to the opposite side and made a sympathetic sound, her fingers hovering over the jagged lines. "These will be tougher. Ink tends to fill in deeper scars. I can create a design to break up the thickness. Both sides would need large designs to cover which will require a couple of sessions to complete. Have you had a tattoo done before?"

"Yeah, on my chest, but I was drunk so I don't remember any pain."

"Thighs are pretty fleshy, so the pain shouldn't be too bad. You'll need to shave prior to getting inked. Going forward, you can continue shaving or let the hair grow over the tattoos."

He hadn't really thought about that part. Shanna turned off the light and moved away so he could stand and yank up his pants.

"The scars are faded and fairly flat so that helps," she said.

He saw the question in her eyes. "I'm ready to move on."

She nodded, holding up her tattooed forearms. "I can relate."

"Thanks for talking with me."

"Sure. If you decide to move forward, I can work up some sketches for you. And even if you decide not to but want to talk, I'm here. I get the feeling we could be friends."

"Me, too." Jared grinned, an odd sense of kinship filling him.

He left the shop and started toward his truck. His heart lurched as he spotted Katie walking down the sidewalk toward him. Knowing she was pregnant and seeing her large, swollen belly were two different things. His chest constricted. They'd always talked about sharing their big life moments together. God, he missed her.

Their eyes met, and he signed hello. Her features hardened, her eyes stormy. She turned and walked in the other direction.

Fuck that hurt. Jared was in a shit mood by the time he arrived home. He wanted nothing more than to go for a ride alone, but he put on his game face and worked with D and Poppy. Afterward, Virge pulled him aside.

"Are we okay?" The other man's somber expression made him feel like shit. He had no business making this man's life more complicated.

"Yeah, sure. But I think we're better as friends."

Virge released his arm, and he missed the warmth. "If that's what you want."

Fuck no.

Jared nodded, dying a little inside at the hurt in the other man's eyes.

Christ, I'm a chickenshit.

Chapter Twelve

The next week passed in a haze. *Friends.* Virge felt a profound loss being near Jared without being able to touch or kiss him. And it wasn't just physical. The cowboy had erected a giant wall around himself. He no longer shared personal stories and started treating him with the same impersonal politeness he would a guest, and Virge fucking hated it.

But he couldn't risk losing Jared completely by pushing for more. D would be devastated. He should be focusing only on his nephew anyway, but late at night he tossed and turned, thinking about Jared until he finally gave in and got up to write. The only plus side was Miranda loved the chapters he'd submitted for her review.

D crawled into his lap one evening and touched his face. "Sad, Daddy Vir?" It nearly broke his heart. So much for keeping his shit together.

"I'm okay. Just tired." He hugged the little boy.

Later that night, he called his mom.

"You sound off. What's going on?"

He sighed. "How did you know dad was 'the one'?"

"I wanted him to be the last person I saw at night and the first I saw the next morning. What happened? I thought things were going well."

"He said he wants to be friends." He tried and failed to keep the bitterness out of his voice.

"Oh, honey. I'm sorry. Don't give up on him. Love isn't easy."

They talked for a while longer before ending the call. Feeling restless, he turned to his nephew who played with toys on the floor. "How about we go out for ice cream?"

D jumped up. "Yay! Ice cream!"

Virge held his hand as they walked down the hallway toward the main lobby, which was packed with people who seemed to turn as one as they approached.

"That's him!" The crowd surged toward them. Flashes went off, briefly blinding him, and he could barely hear over shouted questions. D shrieked, and Virge picked him up. Bodies pressed against him from all sides, and people tugged on his clothes as he shoved through the crowd.

"Mommy! Mommy!" D screamed. *Jesus*. Virge pushed harder, finally making it back to their apartment. People swarmed around them as he opened the door. He slammed it shut and threw the dead bolt.

D sobbed and shook like a leaf. He sat on the couch and rocked him. He could hear people yelling in the hall.

Someone pounded on the door.

"It's Jared."

"Daddy J," the little boy whimpered.

"Stay here, D. I'm going to let him in." He opened the door and quickly closed it after Jared entered, blocking the people trying to peer inside.

"I've called for backup. We're taking you to the ranch. Pack enough stuff for a few days. I'll stay with D."

Virge gathered up their things, mentally trying to remember everything. The remaining Malone brothers arrived with Rafael. The men grabbed their bags, leaving his arms free to carry D. As they exited the apartment, the brothers formed a protective circle around them while Rafael cleared a path. The paparazzi scattered to make room for the pissed-off Dom and the large brothers surrounding them. It was an impressive view on the inside and must have been damn intense from the outside.

"Get in. I'll drive." Jared threw his keys to Nate before commandeering the Subaru. Virge climbed in the back with D, got him buckled into his seat, and rubbed his little arm while his nephew sniffled and clung to Boo Bear.

The Malones caravanned out of town—Wyatt in front, Jared and them next, Nate and Sam following. They drove carefully despite the dumbasses who followed them.

"How did you know?" Virge asked.

"I stopped by the diner. Al, the owner, said a bunch of out-of-towners were asking questions about you. Is it true? Are you Malcolm Stone?"

"Yes."

"You didn't trust me to know?" Jared turned to glance at him. The hurt expression on his face twisted Virge's gut.

"I'm still on the force. Only a few people knew." Which sounded weak given the friendship the Malones, especially Jared, had given him. *Who leaked this?* Anger simmered through him.

By the time they pulled up to the ranch, D had fallen into a fitful sleep. Virge carried him into the house and placed him in the room Jared pointed out. He set the baby monitor on the nightstand so he could use the app on his phone to listen for when D woke up.

When they returned downstairs, Nate seemed ready to explode. "Is Idris Elba going to play you? I asked if you knew anyone famous, and you're a celebrity, too. I know someone famous!"

"Breathe, Nate," Wyatt said.

"Idris is booked up, so he can't play Derek. And while Derek is my creation, I'm not him. Don't forget your brother-in-law is also famous. Being a Pulitzer Prize winning photographer is nothing to sneeze at."

"Rafael? Sure that's cool and all, but he's not like famous-famous."

"It's a good thing I have a strong sense of self." Rafael smirked.

"Do you get to pick who plays Derek? Will you be on set? Do you get to tell them what to do? They'd better not fuck up your books," Nate rattled out.

"I'll do some consulting, but I plan to leave the moviemaking to the professionals." Virge had heard about some authors being divas and wreaking hell on movie sets with their demands. He didn't roll that way.

"When's the next book coming out? I've read them all, and it takes me forever to finish a book, so that's saying something. Tell him, Jared. Tell him."

Nate practically vibrated.

All the brothers nodded in unison, which was kind of trippy to see.

"I'm working on the next one now. No release date scheduled yet. Listen, I need to make some calls."

"We'll watch D if he wakes up before you're done," Gabi said.

"Thanks."

Rafael took him aside. "Do you have a publicist?"

"No, my agent wants me to get one, but Teisha did all my promoting. I haven't been able to bring myself to find someone else. It's stupid, but it feels like replacing her."

Sympathy shone in Rafael's eyes. "I understand. I have a few people you can talk to when you're ready."

Virge clasped the Dom's shoulder and then left the room.

First, he called his captain. It was both easy and hard to officially resign from his job. He then spoke to Miranda, his lawyer, and his mom. Finally, to Social Services since they needed to know their location for possible check-in visits.

Thankfully, dinner had been quiet because Virge had developed a pounding headache. D went to bed early despite his nap. He had nightmares throughout the night, but, by dawn, he slept soundly. Too edgy to sleep, Virge went downstairs. Only to see a shirtless, barefoot Jared storm out the front door with a shotgun.

Chapter Thirteen

"**W**hat. In. The. Hell." Virge pulled back the curtains and peered out the window. Jared stood with the shotgun butt resting on one cocked hip. *Fuck that is sexy.* The cowboy raised his fingers to his lips and gave a piercing whistle.

"Listen up out there. You're trespassing on private property. You have until the count of three to leave, or my brother will flush you out of hiding, and I'll shoot your asses. One...two...." A herd of people popped up from several locations and started running down the driveway, yelling, "Don't shoot!"

Nate joined him on the porch and snickered. "That was fun."

The brothers returned to the house. "As a former cop, do I want to know if you'd really shoot them or not?"

"The gun is old and unloaded," Jared said.

Thirty minutes later, Jared's picture appeared all over the Internet with headlines like *Gay Author's Cowboy Stud Muffin.*

"That's what you get for wrangling paparazzi while half-naked, bro." Nate gave him the *duh* expression. "I can't believe the stupid stuff people are coming up with. They need to check their facts. Says here you're forty-three years old, Virge. No way you're that old."

He flushed. "That's true."

"Damn, son! Hope to look as good as you when I'm older. Oh my God, this one says we participate in orgies. And it's got all our names listed. Even Gabi's. What a bunch of crap." Nate chuckled.

Later that afternoon, he found Nate staring off into space.

"You okay? I'm sorry this has caused so much chaos for the ranch. For all of you."

"No, it's okay. You're our friend. It's good for you and D to be here. Just got some news I hadn't expected."

"Can you tell me?"

"The library can't risk having a rumored deviant reading to the littles, so it's time to hang up my spurs." Nate shrugged a shoulder, but the tightness of his tone showed how upset he was.

"They fired you because of the shit the gossip rags are spreading?"

"Yep."

"That's complete bullshit." Fury filled him. The Malones had done nothing but good for him and D, and now this happened. Virge fished out the notebook where Teisha had written all the passwords to his social media accounts. The world was about to meet the real Malcolm Stone.

Chapter Fourteen

"**O**h my God, Virge, you broke the Internet," Nate exclaimed.

"You're trending," Jared said.

"Is that good?"

Nate held out a tablet and pointed. "See here? There's a video of people protesting at the library. It was awesome for you to stand up for me like that. And look, Samuel L. Jackson tweeted you. *I like your style. You're one badass motherfucker.* How cool is that?"

"Motherfucker. Motherflunker," D chanted and giggled.

Virge and Jared glared at Nate who groaned. "I'm going straight to hell."

After talking to his nephew about good and bad words, he called Miranda.

"Virge, you are the biggest thing on the planet right now! I loved the video, but you really need to work with a publicist."

"My friend Rafael mentioned a few people. I'll call them."

"When?" she asked with the strictness of a drill sergeant.

"Now?"

"Exactly. Tabitha loves the new chapters. Keep them coming." She hung up before he could respond.

He contacted Jackson Wolfe who impressed Virge with his down-to-earth personality and practical strategies. His rates wouldn't break the bank either. Having seen his video, Jackson suggested an interview with Marcus Gold, an up-and-coming openly gay news anchor known for his integrity and fair reporting.

With a whirlwind of activity, they scheduled the interview with the news crew to arrive the next day.

***

Jared stood in the background, his arms folded across his chest. The camera crew had set up in the converted bunkhouse's main room, which they used for large events. Virge sat opposite Marcus Gold, their chairs barely far enough apart to accommodate the author's long legs. Jared gritted his teeth. He hated the reporter's handsome face and the easy smile he pulled from Virge with his witty banter.

"Why are you doing this interview, Virge?" Marcus asked, his expression studious. *Fucking posh British accent.*

"A lot of crazy, untrue things have been said about me in the last few days. I had planned not to respond, but a situation involving a friend of mine has compelled me to speak out."

"Ah, yes, the reading program at the local library." Marcus nodded.

"That's right. The Malones have been nothing but amazing to D and me. They're good people, and nothing being said about them is even remotely true. I couldn't stand by while they're being slandered."

"A man of character like you would do no less. Now, D, he's your nephew, correct?"

"Yes, he's just a little boy and very fragile right now. I ask that the press respect our privacy."

Marcus outlined what had happened to D's mom and admonished all the people who'd ambushed them. Jared's chest tightened. No little kid should have to deal with shit like this.

"And you plan to adopt D?"

Virge nodded. "That's right."

They spoke for another twenty minutes about his books and the upcoming movies. "Thank you for meeting exclusively with us. One last question from one gay man to another, is there any truth that you're in a romantic relationship with one of those hunky cowboy brothers?"

The author chuckled and waved his hand dismissively, which hurt Jared with the force of a punch to the face. "No, they're just good friends."

"You heard it here, folks. The handsome Virge Stevens aka Malcolm Stone is very single."

Good friends. Could he have made a bigger mistake? *You reap what you sow, asshole.* A hand grasped his shoulder, and he half turned to see Nate beside him. Jared tilted his head, silently indicating he was okay, but his brother still looked concerned.

Once the cameras stopped filming and the production staff removed their microphones, Marcus and Virge stood. "Thank you for speaking with me, Virge. We'll add in some footage of you and D and the protest at the library. If you need anything, you give me a call. My personal number is on the back." Marcus handed over his card with a wink.

Jealousy burning a hole in his gut, Jared shouldered past Nate and returned to the house.

Chapter Fifteen

Staying at the ranch, Virge saw Jared was 100 percent genuine cowboy. The man could lasso, worked cattle like a pro, and rode his horse as if they were one. He felt complete awe for the younger man, and, unfortunately, Jared impressed the guests, as well. Both men and women flirted, trying to get his attention. The cowboy never encouraged them, but Virge still didn't like it. Scratch that, hated it. Like now, a woman caressed Jared's biceps as he explained something about the horse she'd selected to ride. His eye twitched, and he wanted her hand off his cowboy *now* and breathed a sigh of relief as Jared eased away from her. But he wasn't his cowboy.... Firmly in the friend zone, he couldn't stake a claim, but he sure wanted to.

Virge turned when he heard his name being called. Sam waved at him from the porch. He half jogged up the stairs. "Is everything all right? Is it D?"

"He's fine. Mitch Dunning left a voice mail on the ranch's line. Seems there's an issue with your apartment."

"Why didn't he call me?"

"Because he's an asshole. Do you have your renter's contract handy?"

"Yeah, it's in my bag."

"Go get it and meet me in the office." Although the quiet one, Sam was clearly made of the same take-charge material as the rest of his brothers.

Virge went upstairs and grabbed the contract. He peeked in on his sleeping nephew before joining Sam.

He stared at the wall loaded with college degrees and other accomplishments while the other man read through the contract. He knew it took hard work and dedication to achieve a higher education, and the fact that all five brothers had done so despite being orphaned said a lot about them.

"I'm not an attorney, but I know my way around contracts, especially ones set in Montana. Are you okay if I call him for you? I'll put it on speaker so you can hear," Sam said.

"Okay." He normally handled things on his own but deferred to Sam's knowledge.

Sam dialed the office phone and put it on speaker.

"Dunning here." The man sounded like he smoked at least a pack a day.

"Mitch, this is Sam Malone over at Blackbird Ranch. I have Virge Stevens on speaker with me. Got your voice mail there's an issue with his apartment. What's up?"

"Vandalism is the last straw. You need to move out now and don't expect to get your deposit back."

"The apartment was fine when I left it," Virge said.

Sam cut in before he could say more. "Mr.

Stevens isn't responsible for any vandalism. He doesn't have to vacate the premises without a written request and a fifteen-day notice per your contract with him. He will leave the apartment, but you will pay him the remainder of his rent for the month and the full deposit when he returns the keys, or he will sic his fancy Hollywood lawyer on you."

Virge repressed a snort, thinking of his unassuming family lawyer.

Mitch sighed. "Fine, just come soon. We can't get rid of the photographers."

He took pity on the guy. "I'll stop by this afternoon."

Sam hung up. "If he gives you any trouble, just let me know."

"But now what do we do? We can't impose on your family much longer."

"Nonsense. You're welcome to stay."

"Then I insist on paying room and board." He glared at the other man across the desk.

Sam rolled his eyes and named a price much lower than the guest rates listed on the ranch's website.

"That's too low. I can't accept that." Virge frowned.

"It's the friends and family discount. Take it or leave it." Sam leaned back in his chair and folded his arms across his chest.

Resisting the urge to roll his eyes in return, he huffed, "Fine. We'll stay."

"Good." Sam smiled big enough to show dimples.

Damn cowboys, all good-looking and smart.

Jared offered to help gather the rest of their belongings while Gabi watched D. As they pulled into the parking lot, the paparazzi rushed them. Virge had never wished for a Kardashian scandal like he did now. Maybe then these photo vermin would leave.

They pushed through the people, ignoring their questions. They entered the lobby and walked down to the apartment. *Go Home* had been spray painted on the door.

Jared scowled and followed Virge inside. He felt numb as he gathered the rest of their stuff and placed it in the SUV. He did a final run through to make sure the apartment and furnishings were in proper order. Jared remained by the vehicle while he turned in the keys.

Mitch quickly handed over his check. "I'm sorry about everything that's happened. Please tell Sam Malone I fully cooperated."

"Thank you. I will."

As he left the apartment building, Ashford pulled up and didn't bother deterring the photo jerks.

"Do you know who damaged the door?" Virge asked.

"No one saw nothing." The deputy smirked. "Sorry things didn't work out for you. Safe travels back to L.A."

"He's staying with me." Jared glared at Ashford, whose smirk morphed into a scowl.

Jared handed over the keys, and they climbed into the Subaru under the deputy's watchful glare. Neither of them spoke as Virge drove out of town. He again pondered who'd discovered his identity and his location. If the person with the right resources dug into his taxes, they'd see his pen name, and someone local would know where he was. Someone like the douchebag cop.

"You and Ashford have history?"

Jared grunted derisively. "It's complicated."

"He's in the closet," he guessed.

The other man nodded. "We were together for a year. I've always been out, but I understood it could cause him trouble with work. I wanted to protect him, but, after a while, I started feeling cheap. I hated being a dirty little secret. Each time I tried to end it, he reeled me back in with sweet talk and promises. I'd learned all about manipulators and abusers in my college psych classes but didn't realize how bad things were until it was over."

Virge frowned. "He hurt you?"

"Not physically, but he was verbally abusive. I suspected he was cheating on me, but he told me I was paranoid and clingy when I confronted him. The reality turned out to be much worse than I imagined."

Fucking gaslighting bastard. He clenched his jaw. "What happened?"

"Two hours after being with me, he publically announced his engagement to my best friend, Katie. Seemed he'd been seeing us both behind our backs for a few months. He'd fed her some bullshit about wanting to be private while he courted her. More special with only the two of them knowing. I tried to warn her about him, but he'd told her I made moves on him and would be jealous. Anything I said would be lies. I didn't have any proof like texts or anything because he used different phone numbers and wouldn't let me use his real name in my contact list. God, I was so stupid."

"Sounds like she wasn't much of a friend if she didn't believe you."

"Katie had it rough growing up. She's deaf, the

one I learned to sign with. She was home schooled after being bullied by other kids. She's never been anywhere but here. Blake used her insecurities and inexperience against her. They got married, and she's pregnant now.

"When he stopped by the ranch the other day, he all but admitted he's using her so he can win the sheriff position next election. The asshole wanted to hook up with me again." Jared touched his lips, and Virge's gut told him the man wasn't telling him everything about that visit.

He barely suppressed a growl. "What a piece of work."

"The worst thing is, I lost my best friend. I worry about her. I feel like I failed her."

"You tried, Jared. She's an adult and can make her own decisions. You've got to let that go." He placed a hand on Jared's thigh. Before he could remove it, the other man twined their fingers together.

He drove in silence for a while, wondering what the contact meant and how long it would last.

"Were you out at work?" Jared asked.

"Yes but low-key about it because, frankly, it was no one's business who I slept with. When I was a beat cop, I volunteered to cover Pride. I'm sure my superiors thought they were very progressive having an openly gay, black man in their ranks."

"Did other cops give you shit?"

"Not really, but I'm legacy so I'm sure that helped."

"Your dad was a cop?"

He nodded. "And my grandpa, too. Both were legends in their own ways."

"You haven't mentioned your dad, only your mom. He's passed on?"

"Yeah, pancreatic cancer. Been gone four years, but I still miss him."

Jared squeezed his hand. "I'd love to hear more about him, if you'd like to share."

Virge's heart swelled at the other man's genuine interest. Some of the men he'd dated only wanted to talk about themselves, were constantly distracted by their phones, or just wanted to have sex.

Virge shared a story about when he was four years old and borrowed his father's handcuffs to try out and lost the key. Jared's laughter broke off when the truck ahead of them veered off the road and slammed into a tree. The cowboy leaped out of the SUV before Virge came to a full stop, racing toward the wreck.

Chapter Sixteen

J ared wrenched open the door, thankful to see the airbag had deployed. "Owen, are you all right?"

"Jared?" His closest neighbor peered at him in confusion. "I don't feel well. Chest hurts." Owen was pale and sweating profusely.

"Stay still. Help's coming."

Virge approached. "I called 911, but they're at least fifteen minutes out."

Jared heard a whimper from the backseat. "Is someone else in the truck?"

"My grandson, Liam."

Fuck. Liam was about D's age. "Hold on, Liam. I'm coming."

"Jared, we need to get them out," Virge said. "It's leaking gasoline."

"You help Owen and stabilize his head and neck the best you can." Jared rushed around to the other side of the truck. He did a quick assessment of the little boy before pulling him from the car seat. Flames burst from under the front end.

"Get back," he yelled to Virge.

They staggered away from the truck and were almost to the road when it exploded.

Owen grasped his chest and collapsed. Jared passed Liam to Virge before crouching down to shake his neighbor. No response. "Owen, don't do this to me. Hang on." After going through the checks, he began CPR.

While fully trained in CPR and other first aid, it was very different to have a real life in your hands. Jared blocked out the fear and let the adrenaline carry him through. An ambulance and the fire truck showed up. He stepped aside to allow the EMTs access. Colby went to work on Owen while Jennifer checked Liam.

"Can you contact their family?" Virge asked.

Jared nodded and reached for his phone.

Chapter Seventeen

Not able to sleep, Virge decided to sit on the porch for a while. Jared stood by the railing, radiating tension.

"Are you okay?"

"Yeah. Owen's wife just called. He's going to make it but has a long recovery ahead of him. I keep thinking about Liam. What if I hadn't gotten him out in time?"

"But you did. That little boy and his grandpa are alive because of you. You're a hero."

Jared made a scoffing sound. "I just did what needed doing. Besides, I wouldn't have been able to save them without you."

Jared could have been seriously injured. The dark thought had Virge pulling the other man into his arms. The cowboy tensed and then relaxed into his touch. Jared raised his head and kissed him. He groaned at the tentative brush of lips but reined in the urge to deepen the contact. The other man wasn't making it easy, pressing his tongue against the seam of his lips. He gasped at the feel of Jared's hardness against him, and the cowboy took that opportunity to plunge in. Their tongues dueled for dominance, and then Jared sighed in sweet surrender.

Virge broke off, panting.

Jared licked his own swollen lips. "Why did you stop?"

"I want to be more. More than just friends, but I'm afraid to mess up again."

"You didn't do anything wrong. It was me."

"Will you tell me about it?"

Jared nodded.

Virge led him to the large porch swing. He sat and pulled the other man down onto his lap. The swing groaned.

Jared chuckled into Virge's shoulder. "Wyatt will have my ass if I bust Mom's swing."

"It'll hold." He'd seen the number and sizes of guests who'd tried out the popular swing. He stroked a hand over Jared's back, waiting for him to speak.

"All of us were hurting real bad when our parents died. I felt invisible and overwhelmed. Like I couldn't breathe sometimes. I didn't want to be a burden. Wyatt had to deal with Brett and with Nate, who went off the rails. Luckily, he didn't end up in juvie. Anyway, I accidentally cut myself and discovered the physical pain dulled the emotional kind. I started cutting myself after that."

Virge stroked his side, not wanting to interrupt. His heart ached as he thought of the teenaged Jared in so much pain he'd resorted to self-harm.

"One day, I cut too deep, and it bled like crazy. I panicked and screamed for Wyatt. I didn't want to die. I'll never forget the devastated look on my brother's face. God, he was so pale. I started seeing

Dr. Sarah."

"She helped you?"

Jared nodded. "After that incident, I wanted to stop. She gave me new coping techniques." He rubbed a hand down his leg. "But I have scars. All over my thighs."

It finally clicked. Jared hadn't rejected him sexually; he hadn't wanted Virge to see his scars.

"We all have scars."

"I'm ugly. Damaged goods," Jared said in a tight whisper.

"You look me right here in my face," Virge growled, and waited until Jared's eyes met his before continuing. "You are the most beautiful man I know, and some scars aren't going to change that. Did Ashford say those things? That you're ugly and damaged?"

Jared nodded.

He cursed. "That man is a spineless idiot. Please don't let his words define you anymore. You're worth a million of him." He kissed the side of Jared's head. "Thank you for trusting me with your story."

"Thank you for understanding." Jared stared at him, his eyes luminous in the moonlight, and their lips met again. The light touch soon grew heated.

Virge groaned. "I wish we could be alone." He silently swore as the other man tensed. "Not because I want to hide you. There are just so many people around, and I want to do *very* non-family related activities with you."

"You do?" Jared asked in a breathy voice.

Virge gave him a final kiss before pushing him gently off his lap. "But only when you're ready." He cupped the other man's chin, running his thumb over his lips. "Good night."

"Good night, Virge."

He returned to the house, while he still had some self-control. The cowboy was just too damn tempting.

Chapter Eighteen

Despite the late night, Virge rose early the next morning with D. The little boy was in a mood. He ripped the clean diaper out of Virge's hands and threw it at his head. He so didn't need this pre-coffee.

"D, come on. The sooner you get dressed, the sooner you can go downstairs and play."

"No!" His nephew crossed his arms and stomped his foot.

"No, you don't want to get dressed?"

"No diaper! I'm a big boy!"

"Oh." *Oh!* "Well, you have underwear in the bag over there. You let me know when you need to use the bathroom, okay?"

"Yes, Daddy Vir."

After D dressed, Virge got him settled in the family room with some toys then went onto the kitchen to start the coffee. While it brewed, he slipped on his readers and skimmed his latest chapter.

"I didn't know you wore glasses."

He glanced up when Jared walked in.

"Only for reading. The hazards of getting older." He laughed sheepishly and reached to remove them only to be stopped by a firm grip on his wrist. His self-consciousness evaporated with the banked fire in Jared's eyes.

"You're like a walking wet dream, Virge. Don't you realize what you do to me?" The cowboy pressed close.

His mouth dried as he stared at the handsome younger man. Jared nuzzled against his jaw before brushing his lips over his ear. He swallowed hard, suddenly tight with need.

The cowboy leaned against him. "I can picture us in bed on a lazy Sunday morning," he murmured into his ear. "You're wearing those glasses and reading me something from your latest story. Something no one else has seen but you. I get so turned on listening to you reading a super racy sex scene in your hot-as-fuck voice that I'd begin to suck you off. Not enough to make you come, but enough to feel really good. You continue to read with me edging you until you can't take it any longer. You'd throw those pages, not caring about the mess you make. Then you fuck me wearing those glasses."

He gasped softly when Jared nipped his earlobe, his groin throbbing.

Virge fucking loved the picture the cowboy painted. He captured Jared's lips in a scorching kiss, losing himself in the other man's heat. Someone coughed loudly, and Jared pulled back. Virge palmed his face, not letting him fully escape. The other man's eyebrows rose, and he pressed a chaste kiss to Jared's lips. "Not hiding." He released him.

Jared smiled, and his eyes brightened. He was so stunning, he took Virge's breath away.

Gabi chuckled. "I was going to say good morning, but I can't top that."

They helped make breakfast, and, soon, Nate joined them at the table.

"So what is everyone planning to do today since we don't have guests?" Gabi asked.

"Jared mentioned wanting to show Virge more of the ranch, so the little dude can chill with me. I figured binge watching a ton of Disney movies and overdosing on sugar...and whatever D wants to do."

Everyone laughed.

"Are you sure? D's declared no more diapers."

"All right, little man!" Nate rounded the table and high-fived D. "Let's go have some fun. How about some *Mario Kart*?" he asked while helping him off the booster chair.

"Remember to play nice, Nate." Jared turned to Virge. "You ready to go?"

"Sure."

"Don't forget the lunch I packed for you," Gabi said with a wink.

Apparently, his day had been all planned. They soon left the ranch, and he stared out the window, admiring the scenery while Jared drove.

"How did you become a writer?"

"I read a lot. Helps to quiet my mind at night. I complained to Teisha about the complete inaccuracies in a story I'd read, and that I could write something a hundred times better. She basically told me to either go for it or shut the hell up. So I took a couple of online writing classes and never looked back."

"Are you going to miss being a cop?" Jared glanced at him briefly.

Virge shrugged. "Yes, in some ways, but the odd hours would have made it tough to raise D. And with writing, I can be located anywhere. I'm financially comfortable now, but if I eventually need a job, I have a number of options."

They pulled off the side of the road and walked about half a mile. He peered out over the ridge to the surrounding valley. "I'm feeling a *Lion King* moment here. Did your dad bring you all up here when you were babies and hold you up like the monkey did?"

Jared laughed. "Naw. Well, maybe he did with Wyatt."

They returned to the truck and drove a little farther. Jared pulled a cooler and blanket from the back and led the way to a grassy bank near a slow-flowing river.

Jared set the cooler down and spread out the blanket. Then he sat and yanked off his boots and socks. The cowboy stood and pulled his T-shirt over his head. "Can you swim?"

"Yeah. Don't have swim trunks with me, though." He glanced from the river to Jared who unbuttoned his jeans.

"Don't need them for skinny dipping," Jared said as he slid the jeans and briefs down his legs.

A flash of heat warred with uncertainty. Virge had only swum in pools. Wading knee-deep in the ocean didn't count. He tried to think if anything deadly or poisonous lived in Montana waters. Damn, he should have done more research.

"Is it safe? I watched this show about this fish that swam right up a guy's...." He shuddered and reflexively covered his denim-clad dick with a hand.

Jared chuckled. "Nothing like that. We do have crawdads, so don't stick your toes in between the rocks."

He placed his hands on his hips. "Is that supposed to make me feel better?"

"I'll keep you safe. Seriously, I've been coming to this spot most of my life, and the worst thing that ever happened was Nate poking me with a stick to scare me."

"Which is one of the many reasons I'm never going skinny dipping with your brother."

He gawked at the fully naked man in front of him, unable to look away from the muscular, sculpted ass and impressive package as Jared stalked toward the water.

The cowboy stepped into the river and glanced back at him. "So are you coming in or what?"

Virge quickly stripped. He walked over smooth rocks, which still hurt the tender soles of his feet.

"There's a ledge, and then it drops off," Jared said before fully submerging into the river.

The river was way colder than Virge expected on a summer's day, and he hissed as the icy water hit his naked balls, but he focused on Jared waiting for him. He stepped off the ledge, completely submerged underwater. Virge gasped and struggled to the surface. He emerged sputtering and floundering.

"Hey, it's okay. I've got you," the other man said, holding him up by his upper arms. He relaxed into the cowboy, knowing he would keep him safe. "Sorry, this was a bad idea. We can get out. No worries." Jared's blue eyes shone, reflecting the sparkling water. His wet hair slicked back, making his cheekbones and jawline more prominent.

"Jared." Virge grasped the other man's waist.

The cowboy groaned and pulled him closer for a kiss. He moved his hands and kneaded Jared's ass as their cocks rubbed together under the surface. Their legs tangled together, but the cowboy kept them from sinking. The slide of their erections and the sexy sounds the cowboy made caused him to ache with exquisite need.

"Virge!" The urgency in Jared's tone cranked him up.

"Yes, that's it. Give it to me."

The other man tensed and came with a groan. Virge's toes curled with the release that slammed through him. They clung together.

"Wow." Jared smiled.

"Double wow."

They kissed but gentler now. Virge glanced at his fingers cradling Jared's face and chuckled. "I'm getting pruny."

"Let's dry off and have some lunch." Jared held his hand as they emerged from the river.

Both lay out on the blanket, warming their naked bodies in the sun.

Virge felt so good. So alive. He rolled onto his side and ran his fingers over Jared's chest, focusing on his tattoo.

"We got really drunk a few years back on the anniversary of our parents' death and ended up getting tattoos that night."

"I like it."

Jared grinned. "I lucked out. Nate ended up with the Superman symbol on his ass."

They laughed but soon stopped, sexual tension

crackling between them as they touched. He moved in between Jared's legs, kissing him long and deep before exploring his chest and down his abs with both hands and lips. In the past, Virge hadn't been a patient lover, his mind often returning to details of the cases he'd been working, which led to restlessness. Now, the only thing that existed was the amazing man beneath him. A man he wanted to map every inch of. He carefully traced the scars lining Jared's thighs with his fingers and met his eyes.

"I thought about covering them with tattoos, but I've come to terms with them."

"You're beautiful just the way you are." He placed a kiss on each thigh then took Jared's dick in his mouth.

The cowboy gasped.

Virge alternated between sucking and swirling his tongue, listening to the other man's verbal responses to learn what he liked best.

"Please, Virge. I want you inside me."

"I don't have—"

"In my jeans pocket."

Virge rummaged around and found the lube and condom. He returned to worshipping Jared's cock as he prepared him with his fingers.

He rolled on the condom, and Jared pulled his knees up. Virge pressed in slowly, inching his way into the other man until he bottomed out. He stilled, the feel of Jared's tight grip challenging his control.

"Move," the cowboy urged.

He set a steady pace and adjusted with Jared's responses. He wrapped the other man's legs around his waist and pumped his hips as the cowboy shouted his pleasure.

Jared came, shooting over his stomach and chest. His blissed-out expression pushed Virge over the edge. After he caught his breath, he withdrew from Jared and settled back into the cradle of his legs, not caring about the sticky mess, and, his weight on his forearms, he kissed the other man. After a few minutes, the hairs on the back of his neck prickled, and his cop instincts kicked in. He sat up and glanced around, listening intently.

Jared rose onto his elbows. "What is it?"

"Felt like someone was watching us." Virge continued to scan the area.

"This is Malone land. No one's around for miles except us and the wildlife we just traumatized. Look at that squirrel. He totally dropped his nut, dude," the other man said, sounding *way* too much like Nate.

"Babe." He stared down at Jared, whose eyes widened either at the use of babe, his tone, or both. "I don't want you to use that voice when we're naked ever, ever again."

Jared smiled. "Promise."

"Good, let's wash off in the river and then eat. I'm starving."

Chapter Nineteen

*T*hank God this is almost over. Jared had never felt more self-conscious in his life as, under the watchful eyes of the townspeople, he assisted with Owen's benefit dinner. Some were friendly and curious while others scowled at him and whispered to each other. He rubbed his fingers over his thigh. Too bad Virge couldn't be here. He'd remained at the ranch to watch D and Olivia.

Jared circled around to the silent auction tables. Virge's book and dinner contribution was a very popular item. *Darn, Mrs. Jacoby upped the amount again. Fuck that.* Thinking about the balance in his bank account, he increased his bid to $5,000.

He helped Nate move the trash out back and returned in time to hear the auction results. He only cared about one item. He won! After giving a check to Gabi and collecting his book, he joined Nate at the front entrance of the school. Damn, he couldn't wait to get home.

Blake staggered through the door, reeking of alcohol, and fixed a red-rimmed glare at him. "You've got a big pair showing your face around here. Where's your big city man? Wanted to tell him he can have my sloppy seconds."

Jared grabbed Nate to prevent him from surging forward.

"But he probably won't want you after he loses that little boy of his."

It was Nate's turn to hold him back. "What. Did. You. Do?"

"Let's just say I have evidence that you are more than just friends," Blake said, using air quotes. *God, what a douche.* "And everyone is going to know."

Katie rushed through the entrance and to Blake's side, her hands fluttering frantically. *"Come home. Come home."*

He shoved her hard, and she slammed into the wall. Onlookers gasped, and Jared ran to catch her before she fell. With no one holding Nate, he decked Blake in the face. The two went down in a heap, exchanging punches until Wyatt pulled them apart.

Jared gathered Katie close.

"Are you hurt?" he signed.

"A little. I'm scared. The baby." Tears streaked down her face.

"I'm taking you to the hospital to make sure you're okay."

"But we don't have insurance anymore."

"Don't worry about it. I'll take care of everything."

***

Gabi and Rafael entered the house. Virge met them in the hallway. He noticed she held his book.

"Sorry no one was interested in the book and dinner." He'd wanted to contribute to Owen's medical care. Maybe he could donate money directly.

Gabi gave him an odd look. "Lots of people bid on it. Jared won."

"Jared? But I'd give him a signed book for free and would have dinner with him anytime."

Gabi rolled her eyes. "Men. You explain it to him. My boobs are about to explode. I need to pump." She shoved the book into his hands and left.

Whoa, TMI.

Rafael grimaced. "Sorry, the evening did not end well."

"What happened? Where are the others?"

"Blake showed up drunk and confrontational. He shoved his wife, and Nate got into a fight with him. Jared took Katie to the hospital, and the rest of the family is at the police station waiting to see if Nate will be charged."

"Shit. Are she and the baby okay?"

"I haven't heard anything yet. I'm heading back to our house."

He looked down at the book. "Wait. What about this?"

Rafael faced him, his dark eyes glittering. "I'm not sure if he was conscious of it or not, but he won to make a statement. That you are his, and he doesn't want to share."

"Oh." Warmth surged through him at the thought of Jared feeling possessive of him. "How much?"

"Five thousand."

That's one hell of a statement.

An hour later, the rest of the family arrived with

good news. Katie and her baby hadn't been injured in the fall, and the police had released Nate without charges.

Virge sat in the family room with Jared.

"Apparently, Blake's been spiraling. First showing up to work late and then not showing up at all. He got fired today and blames me for it," Jared said.

He shook his head. "That doesn't make any sense."

"The man needs help. Katie's scared of him and is staying with her sister. Virge, I have more to tell you." Jared rested his hand on his forearm, his eyes darkened with pain.

"What is it? What can I do to help?" His breath caught. He hated seeing that pain, and he would do anything to make it go away.

"He's the one who told the press about you and vandalized the door. And remember when you thought someone watched us at the river? It was Blake. He took pictures of us and sent them out tonight. He also left an anonymous message on the Child Protective Services hotline accusing you of abandoning D without adult supervision for hours to have sex with me."

"Fuck." Virge clutched his fists, dizzy with anger and dismay.

"I'm so sorry. I never meant to cause you problems. If you lose D because of me, I'll never forgive myself." Jared looked absolutely wrecked.

Virge pulled him close. "Hey, none of that. If it's anyone's fault, it's Ashford's. We didn't do anything wrong. I need to make some calls."

"I understand."

Virge gave him a hard kiss before leaving the room.

Chapter Twenty

Virge's phone rang. "Hey, Mom."

"Your mother's still asleep. This is Auntie Ruth."

"Hi. Are you doing okay?" *And why are you calling me on Mom's phone?*

"I needed to speak to you. I heard on the news that there are sex pictures of you on the Internet. Is that true?"

He rubbed his hand over his hair. "It is, but the person who posted them took them without my knowledge."

"I figured you were too smart to do it yourself. All those young people twerping about every second of their lives and sharing pictures of their unmentionables. I just don't get it. Who wants to stare at someone's wienie?"

Virge bit his lip to hold back laughing.

"So this man of yours, does he treat you right?"

"He does."

"Good. Now your Uncle Reggie and I tried the anal sex a few times. The important thing to remember is lots of preparation. That means lube. Saliva will not do, and, frankly, it's disgusting. So lots and lots of lube."

"Lots of lube. Got it, Auntie Ruth." *Kill me now.*

"Love you. Hope you come home soon. I missed you boys at my party. Not sure how many more of those I'm gonna have."

"Miss you, too. Bye, Auntie Ruth."

He placed his head on the kitchen counter.

"Are you okay?" Nate asked as he walked in.

"I just got sex advice from my ninety-one-year-old great-aunt."

Nate laughed. "That's funny, sorry, dude." He sobered. "I hope Blake gets jail time for what he did. I should have punched him a few more times when I had the chance."

Child Protective Services was all over Blake's report and the posted photos. Virge had been on the phone with his lawyer most of the morning.

"What do you mean they've called for a court hearing? They haven't even bothered to do a site visit since we've been at the ranch. Didn't Ashford refute the report? He confessed to the sheriff he made that call without cause."

"His attorney told me he's in the hospital for psychological evaluation."

"Crap."

"I'm sorry, Virge. The press got wind of the unfit guardian accusation, which pushed CPS into action."

"When do we have to be back in California?"

"The hearing is in three days."

He pinched the bridge of his nose. "That doesn't give us much time to prepare, let alone drive home.

We'll need to leave today."

"I can schedule a flight for you."

"D isn't ready for crowded airports and planes."

They spoke for a while longer. After ending the call, he stared off at nothing as he tried to prioritize what to do next, but his thoughts jumbled around in his head too quickly for him to process.

"You have to leave?"

He glanced up to see Jared leaning against the doorframe. He nodded and rose. Jared met him halfway and wrapped his arms around him. Virge sighed. "I wish you could come with us."

"I'm sorry I can't. We have a large wedding party coming tomorrow."

He felt like shit. Jared didn't need this kind of stress. "It's okay. Just wishful thinking. I know you have a lot of responsibilities here."

"Call, text, whatever you can do, okay?"

"I will." Virge kissed him. "I'd better start packing."

Once D found out they had to leave, he was inconsolable. Not even a video call with Grammy stopped his tears.

Jared joined them carrying a gray and white toy horse that looked like Poppy. He sat on the couch next to where D curled up while Nate settled on the floor nearby.

"I've been saving this to give you, and now seems like a good time."

D glanced at the stuff animal and then at Jared. "Poppy?"

Jared nodded. "That's right." He handed the horse to D, who petted the toy. "Watch what happens when you squeeze the front hoof," he said then demonstrated.

A whinny sounded, and D gave a shaky smile.

"I recorded Poppy so you could hear her any time."

"Thank you, Daddy J." D crawled into Jared's lap, wrapped his arms around his neck, and whispered something in his ear. The cowboy screwed his eyes shut and hugged him close.

"I love you, too," he said in a hoarse voice.

Virge wiped the tears from his eyes.

Nate sniffled loudly. "Stupid dust in my eye."

Chapter Twenty-One

Two days had passed, and even with frequent communication, Jared missed Virge and D like crazy. Virge had made an attempt at sounding normal on their last call, but the next day's hearing weighed heavily on them both. Hanging out in his room to avoid his family's well-meaning but suffocating attention, Jared leaned back against his pillows and stared at the selfie Virge had texted of himself and D with the ocean in the background. Someone knocked on his door.

"Go away, Nate."

"It's Sam."

"Oh, come on in."

Sam opened the door. "Got a call from the preschool saying D left some things behind. Can you go pick them up?"

Jared swung his legs off the bed. "Sure."

"Great. Oh, and Gabi told me to tell you she's making your favorite for dinner tonight."

"I won't be late," he said without much enthusiasm.

He drove into town and pulled up to the school. Entering the front office, he introduced himself, and the director led him to the classroom. Jared stared at the wall of children's art. "My Family" was printed on the top of each sheet, but only one caught his attention. D had drawn Virge, D, and him holding hands. Tears pricked his eyes.

"Here's his extra set of clothes and things," the teacher said, holding up a paper grocery bag.

"Can I take that, too?" Jared pointed to the drawing.

"Oh, yes, of course. We hope D comes back. We loved having him here."

"I hope so, too," he rasped out, a lump in his throat.

Jared left the school and drove home in a daze. He parked and unbuckled his seat belt. Reaching for D's stuff, he came to a halt, staring at the picture. Love and sharp pain swirled through him. He rested his hands and head against the steering wheel as tears streaked down his face, the first time he'd cried since his parents died. God, he missed them so much, and what if they took D away...?

The driver's door opened, and a large hand grasped his shoulder. "Jared, what's wrong?" Wyatt asked.

He handed over the picture in response.

"Come here."

Jared slid out of the truck and into his big brother's arms. "I miss them so much," he got out, his throat tight and scratchy.

"It's got to be hard for you. We all miss them."

"I wish I could be there."

"What's stopping you?"

113

Jared pulled back, wiping the tears off his face. "I'm needed here."

"They need you more."

"But what about the guests? The horses?"

"We'll manage. Brett's coming home for a few weeks, and we can hire more staff if you stay in California longer. Whatever you decide, we're always here for you."

"Yeah?"

"Yeah." Wyatt slapped him on the shoulder. "Now go see Sam. He'll book you an open ticket. Rafael's already given him the info to upgrade you to first class."

Chapter Twenty-Two

Virge sat at the table next to his lawyer. Anxiety ate at his gut, and acid burned his throat. He hadn't slept the night before. He turned and stared at D playing quietly next to his family in the gallery.

"All rise for Judge Vazquez-Fletcher."

He stood along with everyone else in the courtroom as the stern, silver-haired female judge filed in.

"Daddy J!" D shrieked, and Virge whipped around. Jared stood in the back of the room. His heart raced as he took in the man in the suit. Damn, he looked sharp. He grinned at the cowboy, the tension in his shoulders lifting some. Jared raised a hand in greeting before joining Virge's mother who frantically tried to quiet the little boy.

"You may be seated," the clerk directed.

As soon as Jared sat down, D crawled into his lap.

Virge gave the judge his full attention.

"I've read both the lawyers' positions as well as

the many character letters submitted on Mr. Stevens's behalf. Since the minor, Donovan Stevens, is largely nonverbal, I have spoken to his therapists and read his files. I have also reviewed the welfare visit reports submitted by the children's services agencies in both California and Montana. Rather than hearing the lawyers speak, at this time I'd like to interview a few individuals in my chambers."

"Your Honor." The state-appointed attorney stood.

"It's within my discretion, Counselor. First, I'd like to speak with Mr. Stevens."

The bailiff escorted Virge to the judge's room and then stood outside the door.

"Please have a seat. May I call you Virgil?"

"Virge, please."

The judge nodded. "How long have you known Donovan?"

"I've been in his life since he was born."

"I see that you are already his guardian. Why adopt?"

"He's been through so much. I wanted to provide him the full security adoption provides. And when he gets older, he'll understand that I'm all in."

"Why do you think you're the best choice for raising Donovan?"

"D belongs with the family he has left. My mother has health problems. I can offer him love, security, and a good education which is better than putting him in the system. I've seen a lot of ugliness in my career, and I'm sure you've seen your share."

"What about normalcy? You're a celebrity, Virge."

"I don't crave or seek out attention. The press is

already dying down, following some other gossip. We'll remain in Montana while D continues therapy, and then I'll evaluate what to do next."

"This letter from your captain says you've resigned from your position as detective. How will you support yourself and Donovan?"

"I believe my lawyer submitted my financials. I have a large amount of savings, and D has money from his parents' insurance policies. I also have income from royalties, movie rights, and a large book advance."

The judge leafed through the file in front of her. "Yes, I see that here. What are your employment plans?"

"I'll write full-time and take a job if needed."

She held up copies of the sex photos. "And what about this?"

"Those were taken without our knowledge or permission while we were in a fairly remote location on private property."

"Where was your nephew at this time?"

"At the ranch being watched by responsible adults. People I trust. My sex life has nothing to do with my ability to raise my nephew. I would never abandon D."

"This man isn't a distraction from your responsibilities?" The judge eyed him over the rim of her glasses.

"He's a man with more honor than anyone I know. He has been there for D and me when we needed help the most and never asked for anything in return." Virge paused and gulped as awareness hit him like a ton of bricks. "I love him."

"That's all I have to ask you." The judge gave him

a small smile. "Thank you, Virge."

Jared sat up straighter as Virge returned to the table. He tried to interpret how things went by the other man's expression, but his face didn't give any clues.

The judge's clerk entered the courtroom. "Judge Vazquez-Fletcher would like to see Mr. Malone next."

Me?

Virge's mother took D from him. He rose and passed Virge, whose brows drew together in concern. Jared couldn't blame him, he hadn't expected him to show up, and now the judge wanted to speak with him. He wouldn't fuck this up though.

He entered the office and sat in the leather chair next to the judge's large wooden desk.

"Mr. Malone. Glad you could join us today. I'd like to ask you a few questions. They will be very personal in nature."

"I'm here to help, Your Honor. I'll answer anything you ask."

"Do you understand why this hearing was called?"

"Yes, ma'am. Child Services has concerns about Virge adopting D."

"What are your thoughts on this?"

"I understand they have a job to do, but Virge is a wonderful guardian who dropped everything to raise D and seek the best therapy possible. That little boy loves him so much. I can't imagine them apart." Jared's voice cracked at the end, and he stared at the judge's desk.

"What about Mr. Stevens being a new celebrity?"

"He's one of the most down-to-earth people I know. He has already taken several steps to minimize their exposure to the paparazzi."

"Including living at your ranch. Describe what that living situation is like."

"They're staying in the main house, two guest rooms on the second floor. Virge pays the ranch on a weekly basis."

"Where do you sleep?"

"On the third floor, ma'am."

"Did you observe a time when Donovan wasn't supervised?"

"No, Virge was either there or had at least one other adult watch D. He's very careful with his nephew's safety."

The judge set copies of the articles on the desk. "What about these?"

"I'm nobody's boy toy, Your Honor."

The judge raised an eyebrow before placing the photos Blake had taken in front of him. His face heated, but he met her eyes squarely.

"We thought we were alone, and D was being cared for by my family at the time."

"What if I told you it was in the Stevens' best interest if you walked away."

"I tried to stay away, but I love that little boy as if he were my own." Jared swallowed around the lump in his throat. He removed D's drawing from his wallet and handed it to the judge. "And as for his uncle, he doesn't know this yet, but I plan to marry him one day. I would do anything in this world to keep them safe and happy."

"And if they remain in Los Angeles?"

"I'd move here."

"What about your family? Your ranch in Montana?"

"I love my brothers and would visit as often as I could, but Virge and D need me."

The judge handed back the picture. "Thank you for your candidness, Mr. Malone. You may return to the courtroom."

After speaking with Virge's mom, the judge took the bench again.

"In reviewing this case closely, I believe it would be a travesty of justice to separate the minor, Donovan Stevens, from his uncle, Virgil Stevens. It's my decision that the inquiry regarding suitability be closed, and the adoption process may proceed. Thank you all for coming today."

Virge turned and stared at him, his eyes wide. Jared let out a whoop. Virge's family hugged each other and him.

"I can't believe you're here," Virge said, looking a bit dazed.

"Figured the more support you had, the better. I didn't expect to talk to the judge, though. I guess I didn't mess up too bad," Jared said ruefully.

Virge kissed him right in front of his family.

Auntie Ruth fanned herself. "Lordy, that's some smooch!"

Chapter Twenty-Three

Virge's mom and aunts had cooked a celebration feast, and laughter filled the dining room—a sound he hadn't heard in his mom's house since his father died. Kind and gracious, Jared answered all his family's questions. Each woman gave him a not-so-subtle signal they approved of the cowboy. D's ear-to-ear grin raised Virge's spirits after the last three days of hell.

After dinner, he found his mom in the kitchen. "I'm going to take Jared back to his hotel."

His mom smacked him with a dish towel. "Virgil Michael Stevens, you didn't tell me how handsome your beau is."

Thank God my family hasn't seen any of the pictures online.

He grinned. "He's even more beautiful on the inside."

"Mmhmm, and you love him something fierce."

"I do."

"What are your plans now?"

"D still comes first. We'll go back to Montana to

continue his therapy and then we'll see what happens next."

"Well, don't let that one go, whatever you do. I can tell he's a keeper. D's going to sleep here tonight. You need some alone time."

"Mom!"

"Go!"

"All right, I'm going." He kissed her cheek and went to collect his "beau."

Auntie Ruth had Jared cornered, chatting his ear off. The cowboy patiently listened to her. She smiled as Virge joined them. "Off you go, boys. Make sure to use protection."

Virge's cheeks heated, and he hustled Jared out the door and into the Subaru. He sped out of the neighborhood as if demons chased them.

"I'm so sorry about that. She has absolutely no filter. Probably a glimpse of what I'll be like at her age. I can just drop you off at the hotel if you want. You're in the driver's seat. Well, metaphorically that is, because I'm driving." *Jesus, why can't I just shut the hell up?*

Jared's hand landed on his thigh and gently squeezed, and Virge breathed in much-needed air.

"Thank you for driving me to my hotel. I'd like you to come upstairs, but only if you want to."

"Oh, I want to. I can't tell you how much."

Jared had never seen Virge so flustered. It was fucking adorable. But as they walked down the hallway leading to his room, Jared's nerves flared up. His hand shook slightly as he swiped his room card in the reader. He muttered a curse as it glowed red with each attempt. Virge pressed against him and covered his hand. They slid the card in together.

Jared sighed in relief as the fucking light turned green. Virge chuckled softly and opened the door before nudging him inside.

Virge pulled him into a tight embrace. Not a polite hug, but a full-on bear hug. "God, I missed you."

Jared released a breath. I missed *you,* not I missed your mouth or your ass as Blake would have said. After being objectified by his ex, hearing Virge say "you" meant everything. He fell in love with him just a little more, something he hadn't thought possible.

"Missed you, too." Jared stroked his back.

"I'm so glad you came. Will you let me love you?"

"Yes." Forever, he wanted to say, but it was too soon for that.

They yanked off their clothes and climbed onto the bed, kissing and touching as if they hadn't seen each other in years. Jared rolled so he covered Virge's body with his own, rubbing their erections together as they kissed. He moaned, it felt so good. Jared fumbled for the lube, slicked up his fingers, and began prepping himself.

"Damn, that's hot." The other man watched him intently.

Jared secured a condom over Virge's erection. He positioned himself and eased onto it. He gasped as it breached his fluttering hole and continued down. The other man grasped him tightly around the hips. "You feel so good."

He began to move, fucking himself on Virge's cock. After a while, the other man sat up while still inside Jared.

"I need to kiss you," Virge groaned.

They kissed long and dirty as Virge guided him up and down. Jared shouted as his orgasm hit hard enough for white to flash before his eyes.

"Yes!" Virge exclaimed, climaxing as well, his warm seed filling the condom inside him.

Later, Jared loved the sixty-nine position with Virge, and they both got each other off "washing" in the shower. They stumbled back to bed. Floating in a sexual haze, Jared fell asleep in his arms.

Virge woke up pressed against Jared. He couldn't remember the last time he'd actually slept with another man and knew it had never resulted in this strong sense of peace.

He feathered his fingers through Jared's soft hair. His heart belonged to this man. But how long would it last? How long before Jared grew tired of his old ass and left?

Jared turned over, nestling into Virge's neck. "That's a mighty lot of thinking you're doing," he said, and Virge shivered as his lips brushed his skin.

"Sorry. Didn't mean to wake you."

"I'm normally up with the chickens. Must have been worn out." The cowboy chuckled, his hand caressing along Virge's chest. "What were you thinking about?"

"The future. I know I'm a lot older than you, and you might not—"

"Look me right here in my face." Jared pulled away. He met his eyes and fought back a grin at Jared, using his own words on him. "I don't care that you're older than me." The cowboy flung off the blanket and climbed out of bed. He stalked over to his clothes. Virge sat up, wanting to punch himself in the face. *Way to fuck this up, asshole.*

Jared fished out his wallet from his jeans and returned to the side of the bed. He thrust a folded piece of paper at him. Virge unfolded it, and a lump formed in his throat. Two tall stick figures held the hands of a small stick figure between them. D had drawn them together. The top of the paper said "My Family." Tears welled, and the drawing became blurry. He glanced up at Jared, who managed to pull off both a fierce and tender expression.

"This is what I want, Virge. I want you and D to be my family. I love you."

He pulled Jared down onto the bed and into his arms.

"I love you, too."

Epilogue

Two months later....

Married. Jared rubbed the ring with his thumb, the weight of the platinum band still unfamiliar. He had a husband, a son, and a whole new set of relatives.

Virge glided across the dance floor with his Auntie Ruth. He still looked dapper in his suit while Jared had ditched the jacket and tie and rolled up his shirt sleeves as soon as the reception started. Which left him open to Nate's sneak pinch attack.

"Ouch!" Jared rubbed away the sting from his arm. "You promised to behave." He glared at his brother, who grinned mischievously.

"I am. If I was misbehaving, I would have given you a titty twister."

"Keep those pinchy fingers to yourself. Why are you bugging me anyway? Why aren't you chatting up the ladies? Gotta be prime hunting grounds for you," Jared said, glancing around the crowded room.

"You looked about ready to float off into space.

Figured you needed grounding."

"If I say I'm perfectly grounded, will you leave me alone?" Jared's affectionate clasp of his brother's shoulder belied his snarky tone.

"What, no room for me now that you have a fancy Hollywood name, Mr. Malone-Stevens?"

"We chose that so D would share both our names when the adoption is finalized."

"Should have known you had a sensible reason, but the boy's got a name bigger than he is."

"He'll grow into it."

"Don't have any doubt about that, especially since he has the best uncle in the world."

Jared groaned. "D and Olivia are going to be spoiled rotten. Plus, you'll be funding their college educations with the swear jar."

Nate chuckled evilly and slapped his back. "I'm real happy for you, bro."

"This will be you one day."

"Oh, probably not. I don't think I'm one to settle down." Nate stared down at his boots.

"Nate—" Virge strode to them. "I'd like to claim my husband for this dance."

His breath caught. *God, I love this man.*

"Excuse me," Jared said to his brother. Virge took his hand, leading him to the dance area, as the first notes of John Legend's "All of Me" began.

He leaned into Virge as they danced, a perfect fit.

As they turned, Jared glanced at Gabi and Katie sitting with their babies. He smiled. Not only had Katie returned to his life, she'd found a solid friend in Gabi. D sat next to them on the floor with his stuffed animals and his new pet, Sunny, a yellow lab puppy Brett had rescued.

"I'm so proud of how D did today, especially with all the people," he said.

"He's come a long way, and so have I. I hadn't even realized how closed off I'd become until I met you."

Jared pulled back and smiled gently. "And you helped me find the courage to love again."

Virge's eyes smoldered. "Can we leave now?"

Jared chuckled and kissed him.

"I love you, babe," Virge rasped as their lips parted, their foreheads resting together.

"Love you, too, and I'll show you just how much tonight. I hope you packed your reading glasses."

His husband growled. "Tease."

"Oh, no, sir. I'm fully committed to following through."

"Then it's a good thing I also packed that new chapter I've been working on."

"Hot damn, I'm one lucky son of a bitch."

"We both are." Virge grinned.

The song ended, and they walked to D.

"Daddies, look! Love you!" The little boy formed the "l love you" sign with his hand.

Jared glanced at Katie who smiled as Virge scooped D up in his arms, puppy and all. "We love you, too."

He returned the sign to his new son then kissed the top of his head, Sunny licking him in the process.

Life was perfect.

About the Author

V.S. Morgan has lived all over the US but calls Minnesota her home now. She's been writing stories since she could hold a pencil and dreams of happily ever afters - even for two hot men - because love knows no boundaries. V.S. writes IRMC contemporary, paranormal, and suspense m/m and m/f with heart.

Also by V.S. Morgan

The Gift

Hunter's Mark

Sam's Temptation